The Rocking Chair
REBELLION

ETH CLIFFORD

The Rocking Chair
REBELLION

Houghton Mifflin Company   Boston

Library of Congress Cataloging in Publication Data

Clifford, Eth, 1915-
  The rocking chair rebellion.

  SUMMARY: A teenager chronicles her involvement with
the residents of Maple Ridge Home for the Aged and their
revolution.
  [1. Old age—Fiction] I. Title.
PZ7.C62214Ro   78-14834
ISBN 0-395-27163-0

AL 10 9 8 7 6 5 4 3

For the young in years and the young in heart in the hope that
this book helps build a bridge between them
and for my cherished niece Andrea
to keep a promise.

The Rocking Chair
REBELLION

Chapter One

Mrs. Humphreys — she's my English teacher — Mrs. Humphreys always says, "Lay the foundation! How are readers going to know what is going on if you don't lay the foundation? The most beautiful house in the world starts with the foundation."

I can just see her now, writing those words on the chalkboard and underlining them the way she does, making that scratchy sound that makes my skin crawl, saying, "Foun–day–shun! Foun–day–shun!"

It was my sister Lissie who insisted that I explain what really happened because the reporter from the *Star* got the facts mixed up — about the turtle race and the Rocking Chair Rebellion and just about everything else.

"After all," Lissie told me, "you're the only one who can tell the whole truth about it all."

Lissie and I don't agree about a lot of things (and it isn't only because I'm fourteen and she's going on eighteen), but this time I thought Lissie was right.

First, though, I'll have to do what Mrs. Humphreys says — lay the foundation so you can understand how I got involved with Mr. Pepper and then with Mrs. Sherman at the Maple Ridge Home in the first place and how I happened to get my Dad's Jaguar smashed.

See, my Dad and I were in the car — my Dad was going to the bank and I wanted to go shopping, so he was giving me a lift, even though he warned me I'd have to find my own transportation home because he was going straight downtown after he went to the bank because he had to show up in court.

And on the way to the bank my Dad and I got to talking about this news item, about this lady whose car got stuck in the snow, and she went from house to house, at night, on a dark lonely road, begging someone to help her, and no one would open the door.

"Shocking!" my Dad said. "Absolutely shocking. To think no one would lift a finger to help her. The trouble is, Opie, people just don't *care* anymore."

So I told him I didn't think it was because people didn't care, it was more like people are afraid, you know? "People just don't want to get involved, that's all, Daddy."

"That's why the world is in the condition it's in," he snapped, getting what my Mom calls his pinched-lip look. "Everyone looks away, and pretends not to see what is happening, as if that will make a bad situation go away ..." He turned his head and looked at me. "I hope," he said, "that no daughter of mine would turn away from someone who needs help. In fact, Opie, I hope you'll consider very seriously what I was discussing with you the other day, a career in social work."

I didn't answer. Ever since I turned fourteen and went into my last year at Northview Junior High, there's been this kind of running battle between my Mom and Dad about my future. Dad is sold on my becoming a social worker — "Involvement, Opie," he keeps saying. "You've got to become involved." My Mom is just as bad in her way, even though she isn't interested in what she calls the "social issues." She wants me to be an English teacher just because she still loves teaching English, even after all these years. Sometimes I think I'll *explode,* the way they keep after me.

Well anyway, by now we were at the shopping center and my Dad dropped me off and he went into the bank. I could see him standing there, fuming at the end of this long line which always comes as a surprise to him even though he knows Friday is the busiest day of the week. My Mom is always saying, "Now, Chet, why do you persist in going to the bank on Fridays and then rant and rave about the long lines and why can't people who have banking problems come on another day? Why can't you?"

"I happen to be a very busy man," my Dad says. Which is true, but he also happens to be a man with a short fuse, which is what Lissie tells him whenever they get into an argument.

So there he was, moving at a snail's pace in the bank, looking at his watch every thirty seconds, and practically pawing the ground like an angry bull.

Would you believe that I went into the five-and-ten and got this absolutely stunning pair of red earrings to go with my new red sweater, and then went into the drugstore and tried out some of the perfumes until the cosmetics lady came over and asked me in this cold nasty voice if I was looking for something special, and when I came past the bank again my Dad was still on the line? There was only one person ahead of him, a lady with a little boy, so I guessed he would be coming out pretty soon.

I turned around and I just happened to see this car with this man sitting at the wheel, and he had the motor running. And I noticed he kept looking at the bank, so I figured he was waiting for the lady with the kid and that he wasn't any more patient than my Dad is. And then, all of a sudden, I remembered that when my Dad got out of the car he had left his keys in the ignition. So I went over to the car, and sure enough, there were the keys. I got into the driver's seat and was just about to take the keys out.

Of course I have a way to go yet before I can get my beginner's license, but I know a lot about cars. My Dad used to take me out on country roads early Saturday mornings and let me take the wheel so I would get confidence. We'd crawl along about ten miles an hour, but at first it felt as if we were flying. And he made sure I knew about the ignition and the brakes and how to go left and right and all. "In case an emergency arises someday," he used to say. "One never knows."

Anyway, I was just about to take the keys out when there was my Dad coming out of the bank, along with this lady and the small boy; and there was this man walking beside them, and he had a gun in one hand and a big sack in the other. I thought I'd just die! I mean, I've seen this exact same thing on TV and in the movies, but this was REAL LIFE.

My Dad started to say something to the man and the man poked his gun real hard and I could see he hurt my Dad. People on the sidewalk were backing away, yelling, "He's got a gun!"

The man with the gun looked back and he shouted

something to the guard standing in the doorway of the bank. Meanwhile he was pushing his hostages toward the curb. That's what the newspapers said later, hostages.

"To ensure a safe getaway, the bandit held three hostages, 44-year-old Chester Chadwick Cross, a prominent Indianapolis attorney, Mrs. Elizabeth Zimmerman, a 27-year-old housewife, and her seven-year-old son, James."

That's exactly what it said, right on the front page of the *Star*.

There they were, sort of coming right toward me. And then I understood what was going to happen next. The man who kept staring into the bank while his motor was running was waiting in the getaway car!

Well, somebody had to do something. My Dad was right. You have to get involved. I mean, would you just sit there and let those robbers force your father into their car at gunpoint, and hold him for ransom probably, and maybe even kill him, because you know you can't trust kidnappers to keep their word, even if they promise to return their victims unharmed?

I just did what I had to do, that's all. I put the key back in the ignition, but I couldn't reach the gas pedal so I had to adjust the seat, and meanwhile out of the corner of my eye I could see them all getting into the car, and the car screaming away from the curb. There was only one thing for me to do. So I did it.

I was scared, all right. My heart was knocking a hole in my chest I was so scared. But I chased after the car — my Dad's car has a real tremendous pickup; you know what those sports models are like . . . *zoom!*

It was like one of those crazy chases you see in the movies. There I was, zipping along on the wrong side of the road, because other cars were pulling out of the parking lot, too, and getting between me and the getaway car. The cars kept swinging out of my way, and the drivers yelling at me and honking their horns like mad. Then this one car came along just as I caught up to the getaway car, and hit me. I went round and round and smashed into the car with the bank robbers in it. And there we all were, tangled up.

I just sat there trembling all over, and now I know what they mean when they say your blood just turns to water.

I was sitting there trying to catch my breath when I saw my father getting out of the other car, only now he had the gun, and he was ordering the two robbers out of the car. They came out looking like ghosts. My Dad made them stand against what was left of their car, with their legs spread out and their hands up on top of the car, and then I heard my father say, "I'm making a citizen's arrest."

And you know, it's not true what they say about a policeman never being around when you need him, because you never saw patrol cars coming so fast, with the sirens screaming and the lights flashing. They took right over; of course my father handed the gun to them as soon as they got there.

Talk about confusion! The lady hostage, Mrs. Zimmerman, was babbling about what a hero my father was and at the same time was practically begging the policemen to let her get her hands on those vicious savage brutes who would frighten a woman and a small child half to death. And meanwhile the lady in the other car was having hysterics and shouting that she was going to sue. It was just a miracle, she claimed, that she and her husband were still alive after what they'd been put through, and that child — and she pointed at *me* — was a positive menace and ought to be put away before she killed somebody. Irresponsible hopped-up teen-ager, she called me, giving me a look that would make King Kong shrivel up. What my poor parents must be going through she just hesitated to imagine! *ME!* And all I was trying to do was to save my very own father and keep those robbers from getting away, which is what I did.

Just then my Dad came over, looking as pale as I felt, and he asked me, "Are you all right, Opie?"

I said I was, I guessed, and asked him the same thing. Then I said, in kind of a small voice, because now he was looking at his car, "I guess you can't say that a daughter of yours turns away when someone needs help."

My Dad was still looking at his car with that stunned expression on his face. I think it's pathetic the way some men become attached to their cars. I mean, after all, they're only machines. Of course, my father talks about his car as if it's human, calls it a she, like "she rides smooth as silk," or "she's a beauty," that kind of thing. I wouldn't be surprised if he sang to it. Once Lissie borrowed the car, and my father spent the whole evening deep breathing and peering out the window ... anyway, I have to be perfectly honest. My Dad's Jaguar was totally demolished.

I gave my Dad the keys and he bowed his head over them, like he was saying a silent prayer. Then he took one of those deep breaths I was telling you about and kind of moaned and he said, "Penelope." I shrank back, because whenever my father uses my whole name I know something's coming I'm not going to like.

"Penelope," he said. "I very much appreciate what you tried to do ... did. You were resourceful and quick thinking and yes, heroic." Just as I was beginning to feel pretty good, he went on, "However, you took a terrible foolhardy chance. You might have been killed."

Why is it when parents are concerned about you they always sound so mad?

I don't have to tell you that my Dad never got downtown. We got a ride home, and after that the house was in a frenzy of activity, what with the police coming to get my Dad's statement and then mine, and the insurance man about the car, and reporters wanting to interview us and take pictures, and the telephone ringing and ringing and ringing ...

Lissie loved the excitement and she talked to the reporter as if she'd been there herself, but I didn't care. Later it was strange to read about myself in the paper, especially the part where Lissie was quoted:

... the vivacious, pert senior at North Central said of her sister, "Opie (Penelope Cross is Opie to her family and friends) is like that. When she starts something, she finishes it, no matter what." In talking to Opie, one finds that she is bright, articulate, with a positive attitude and an honest, open personality ...

Like I said, that was much later. But right then I was exhausted. My Mom said it was the reaction, and that night she talked me into going to bed right after supper. I was glad to stretch out on the bed to get some peace and quiet. I lay there, staring up at the ceiling. That blank ceiling was like a screen — everything that had happened was projected up there — the bank thieves coming out with my Dad, the wild race, the smash.

I thought that was the end of the matter. I didn't know that this one incident was going to lead me off into a whole new direction in my life, because if I hadn't fallen asleep so early, I probably wouldn't have wakened in the middle of the night and seen what I did.

But all I knew then was that I was staring at the ceiling and then my eyes got heavy and I fell asleep. The last thing I remembered was the look on my Dad's face when he saw the Jaguar.

Chapter Two

I must have slept for hours. I suppose that's why I woke up around one in the morning. My eyes popped open and just refused to close again. I don't know why I got up out of bed — restless, I guess — and stuck my head out of the window. There's nothing to see except the lawn and our driveway, and the Pepper house next door.

Everything was so quiet; even the leaves were absolutely still. Our plum tree was in full bloom and where the moonlight touched the small clusters of white blossoms they took on a faint, almost ghostly, glow. I'm telling you all this because Mrs. Humphreys says background is very important. Setting the scene, she calls it.

In some of the books we've been reading in school, there are these characters that get up at night and feel they're all alone in the world and then they have these deep thoughts. I could lie and tell you I was having deep thoughts, too. Only I wasn't. I wasn't thinking about anything, except maybe I wished I could fall asleep again. I just hate being the only one up when everyone else is sleeping.

Well, I yawned and was just about to pull my head in when I caught a glimpse of someone moving along the driveway, sneaking along furtively, carrying something real heavy, because whoever was down there was pulling this thing along, making small, shuffling sounds on the blacktop. Then a figure came out from the shadows, and in the moonlight I could see him clearly. It was old Mr. Pepper from next door. He stopped and stared up at the plum tree. I kind of moved back. Mr. Pepper has always loved that old tree, which is why my Dad never cut it down, though every once in a while, when the plums start to fall, he swears up and down he will. But I know my Dad. He won't. Not as long as Mr. Pepper is next door.

Mr. Pepper didn't see me. He was just standing there, drinking in that plum tree so quiet and beautiful in the moonlight. There was something very sad and private about Mr. Pepper, the tree, and the lateness of the hour. I was going to move away from the window — I felt like such an *intruder* — but then I saw Mr. Pepper shrug his shoulders, stoop down, and pick up a suitcase. That was what made those shuffling sounds, the suitcase being dragged along the driveway.

It bothered me. What was Mr. Pepper doing leaving the house, all alone, with that big suitcase at that time of night? Where was his daughter-in-law, Edith? There are just the two of them now since Mr. Pepper's son Norris died last year. I don't know why this strange feeling came over me all of a sudden. I just knew I had to race downstairs, out of the door, and over to the driveway. Which is what I did. I didn't stop to think about it — I might as well tell you right now that I'm impulsive. Well, you probably figured that out from the way I acted at the bank and all. I started to yell, "Mr. Pepper. Mr. Pepper."

He stopped short. "What are you doing up at this hour? Fourteen-year-old girls should be in bed, getting their beauty sleep."

"Mr. Pepper. Where are you going this time of night?"

"Go back to bed, Opie. This doesn't concern you," he told me. His voice sounded very tired.

"Please, Mr. Pepper." I tried to grab his suitcase. Something was wrong, but I didn't know what. After all, Mr. Pepper certainly didn't have to ask anybody's permission to be outside with his suitcase. I mean, he *is* a grownup.

Jut then my Dad came running over. He was in his pajamas and tying his robe on. His hair was standing up and his eyes still looked glazed with sleep. "What's going on?" he asked irritably. "You went down those steps like a thundering herd of buffalo. Haven't we had enough activity for one day?" He caught sight of the suitcase and stopped talking for a minute. When he spoke again, you'd never know it was the same man.

"What's up, Simon?" he asked Mr. Pepper, very gently.

"Why can't people leave me alone?" Mr. Pepper tried to snap but his words came out all trembly. He ran the back of his hand over his cheeks, like kids do when they've been crying.

I don't know how my Dad did it, but in a little while he had coaxed Mr. Pepper into our house. My Mom came down and then Lissie. Lissie made coffee, and there we were, sitting around the kitchen table, with Mr. Pepper pouring out his troubles.

"She's putting me in Maple Ridge," he said. "Edith is putting me in the Home for the Aged. None of this would be happening if my son Norris was still alive." His voice broke, and he put his head into his hands.

"That's terrible!" Lissie said, with tears in her eyes. She's like me that way; she just can't stand to see someone cry. "Daddy, isn't there something you can do?" she asked.

My Mom and Dad glanced at each other and I thought — they knew! They've known for a long time. I understand those looks by now. Well I should, after fourteen years of seeing them. My Mom got up and went to the telephone. Mr. Pepper didn't even notice. In a little while my Mom was talking in a very soft tone, but I heard her say, "It's all right, Edith," a couple of times so I guessed Mrs. Pepper would be coming over to our house in a while. Mom hung up and slipped back into her chair, just giving my Dad a little nod.

Mr. Pepper lifted his head and looked straight at my Mom. "I expect you and Edith have talked it all out. Agreed that Maple Ridge is best for me." He pressed his lips together. "You haven't come to it yet." I was surprised at how bitter he was when he looked at my Mom, as if she had anything to do with it! "You don't know what it's like. I'll die first. I'm leaving. There's no use trying to talk me out of it."

"Where will you go, Simon?" my Dad asked in that same gentle voice he'd used out on the driveway.

Mr. Pepper's hands started to shake. He clenched them together and put them in his lap and then shook his head.

"What difference does it make? Anywhere. Some place. No matter."

It struck me all of a sudden. He was running away! Old Mr. Pepper was running away from home like a little kid!

"We'll miss you, Simon." I stared at my Dad. I just couldn't believe it. It sounded to me like he was just going to sit there and let Mr. Pepper go off.

"I'll miss you, too. All of you. This place has a lot of memories for me." His head began to nod, the way it always did when he was getting ready to tell me a story when I was a little girl. "You won't cut down that plum tree when I'm gone, will you, Chet?"

"You have my word." My Dad carefully avoided looking at my Mom when he made the promise because he just knew her eyes would be flashing lightning. That tree has been the bane of her life. Plums falling down on the driveway and getting all squashed, the pits digging into the tires. Honestly, the arguments they've had about that tree! But my Dad can be real stubborn about things. I mean, just because Mr. Pepper likes to look out his bedroom window at our tree . . . after all, my Mom and I are the ones who are always cleaning up the mess on the driveway.

Mr. Pepper turned to me, shaking his head. "Do

you remember the day I made the leprechaun tree for you, Opie?"

"It's still there in the backyard, Mr. Pepper." Isn't it funny how things change? That leprechaun tree was the most important thing in my life once. Of course, I was only five years old at the time. I guess the last thought I ever gave that tree was about three years ago, when I fixed it up for Marvin. Marvin is a little kid who lives next door to us on the other side of our house.

"You wanted to have that tree cut down, Chet." My Dad nodded but he didn't say anything. I could see he wished Mr. Pepper would get off the subject of trees, but once Mr. Pepper gets rolling on a topic, he just keeps right on going. "Get rid of the old. Make way for the young. That's the way things go."

My Mom opened her mouth, then closed it again. She looked at the doorway, hoping, I guess, that Edith Pepper would come bursting in.

Mr. Pepper didn't notice. "I can see that tree like it was only yesterday. The trunk in front all worn away, but the branches still trying so hard to leaf. And then I got this idea when I was painting our back door. Opie was watching me. You always did tag around, Opie."

"And then you came over to our backyard and started to paint the trunk of the tree," I said, to show him I really did remember but also, I have to admit, to kind of hurry him a little. It takes old people such a long time to get a story told.

"You asked me what I was doing." Mr. Pepper leaned back in his chair and smiled. "And I told you I was painting a door. It didn't look much like a door to you at first, did it, Opie? Then I painted hinges on the left side, one toward the top and one toward the bottom of the trunk."

With all this reminiscing, Lissie began to get carried away, too. "Remember the door handle you nailed on, Mr. Pepper? You gave Opie a little can of silver paint and let her paint the door handle. Remember that, Opie?"

"You even got me interested in it," my Dad admitted. "I came out afterward and painted the swirls in the handle black, and then I got some wood trim and glued it on." My Dad laughed. "I tell you, Simon, when it was done, and you told Opie to watch for leprechauns to come through that door, I half believed they would myself."

"Lissie," my Mom said. "Maybe you'd better go get Edith Pepper." She was getting restless. It seemed like Mrs. Pepper was sure taking her own sweet time getting over to our house. My Mom kept looking at the clock. She's really a very sociable person, but I could see that sitting in the kitchen over coffee at this time of night wasn't her idea of great entertainment.

"You know Marvin didn't even know what leprechauns are?" Mr. Pepper couldn't believe what I said.

"You're joking!"

"No, honestly! When he was four years old and he was in our backyard, he asked me why the tree was painted and I told him it was my leprechaun tree and he wanted to know what a leprechaun was."

"Why should he know?" my Mom put in impatiently. "You know how Mrs. Goldsmith is. Very matter-of-fact and realistic. And that's how she's raising her son." My Mom's kind of that way herself. She never did take to that painted tree. "Fortunately," I heard her tell Mrs. Goldsmith once, "it's hidden in the back."

Personally, I think fairy tales are good for little kids, especially a kid like Marvin, who never gets to read them. Of course I told him about the leprechauns. Irish elves, I explained to Marvin. Elves that looked like little old wrinkled men, full of mischief. And I told Marvin how if he ever caught one, the leprechaun would have to give Marvin his crock of gold. And Marvin's eyes kept getting bigger and bigger. And then I couldn't get him to go home because he was going to sit and wait for the leprechauns to come out through that door.

"Did they? Come through that door?" Mr. Pepper was smiling.

"I explained and I explained that it was all pretend, that even though there was a painted door on the trunk, it was only an old dying tree ..." I stopped short because Lissie was giving me one of her all-time glares.

I thought maybe I really had said something awful because Mr. Pepper's smile was gone and he looked really grim. And then I heard Mrs. Pepper's voice.

"Dad," she said, from the kitchen doorway. "Chet and Elizabeth would like to get to bed, I'm sure. Please come home now."

"I have no home," Mr. Pepper said, and turned his head away.

"Please, Dad. We've been through all this," she pleaded.

"Come and sit down, Edith. Lissie, is there any coffee left?" That was my Dad, taking charge again. "I think you'd better go to bed, Opie."

"No," Mr. Pepper said strongly. "Let the child stay. Let her learn now what the facts of life are for an old man."

"We've been over and over and over it." Edith Pepper sounded completely hopeless. She was sitting and stirring her coffee, the spoon going round and round till I thought the sound of it scraping the bottom of the cup would just about drive me wild. I guess my Dad couldn't stand it either because he reached over and took the spoon out of her hand. She didn't even notice. "Now that Norris is gone, the house is just too big for two people. With Jim settled in California (Jim was her son) and Dorothy living in England (that was her daughter — Mrs. Humphreys says you must always identify your characters. I don't know how writers do it. It just slows me down something fearful), it's just too much house. Anyway, Dorothy's asked me to come and stay with her, now she's going to have a baby..." She gave her father-in-law a defiant look. "And I want to go. A mother wants to be with her daughter at a time like this."

"I understand all that," Mr. Pepper said. "I don't hold it against you. It's just... what happens to me?" He sounded so frightened and lost, Edith Pepper began to cry. "What can I do?" she asked. "Dorothy only has this tiny house..." She swallowed hard.

"And Maple Ridge isn't as bad as you think it is, Dad. You'll have people your own age to talk to . . ."

"Don't start that 'people your own age' bit again," Mr. Pepper bristled.

I looked at them, sitting around the table. Four grownups, five if you want to count Lissie, and not one of them able to solve the problem.

I suppose if you're an author and making up a story out of your head, you can put your characters into any kind of terrible situation because then you have the power to write them out of it again. But this wasn't a story. It was really happening in our kitchen, and nobody knew what to do. Except bow to the inevitable. I didn't say that. My Dad did. It was awful but that was how it was going to be. Because where could old Mr. Pepper go?

"Do they know I'm coming?" Mr. Pepper asked.

Edith Pepper nodded. "With the house sold and all . . . next week. I'm flying to London the day after you . . . the next day."

Mr. Pepper stared at his hands. "Then I'll truly be alone."

"I'll write to you regularly. You know that, Dad." She tried to take one of his hands but he pulled away. "And when the baby comes, I'll be sending you pictures."

"Truly alone," Mr. Pepper repeated.

"Nonsense," my Dad said briskly. "You'll be visiting with us. And we certainly will be visiting you."

Mr. Pepper looked at me. "And will you come to see me, too, my little leprechaun girl?"

Well, that did it. I mean it really did. I got up, threw my arms around him, and said, "Of course I will. Regularly. I promise."

Mr. Pepper took out his handkerchief and blew his nose. "I'm an old fool, getting everybody all worked up like this. You don't have to promise me anything, Opie. A girl like you, a million things to do. Enjoy the brightness of your youth. All of you . . . you, too, Edith. I apologize. I'm scared, that's all. Forget it. The water in the pool only feels icy in that first plunge. Afterward . . ." he waved his hand, "the water's fine."

I had a picture, suddenly, of the way it used to be, when Mr. Pepper first came to live with his son and daughter-in-law when his wife died. How kind he was, telling me stories, letting me follow him wherever he went, watching him paint and repair things around the house, always patiently explaining. And that magic day when he took an old tree and turned it into a hideaway for leprechauns.

"I *will* come to see you. You wait and see," I told him."

And I meant it too.

So that's how I happened to get involved with the Rocking Chair Rebellion at Maple Ridge, which I will tell you about in a minute.

Chapter Three

The Maple Ridge Home for the Aged isn't far from where we live, and I must have gone past it a million times although I never went inside. It's a great big old mansion, the kind you find sitting well back from the street on lots of scrubby lawn. It's down on Central. My Dad says when the Bearley family owned it, the house was practically in the country. Then the city grew up around it. Some of the other mansions were torn down, and some of them were converted into apartments and some into multiple business offices. The Bearley house sort of went to seed; after a while the windows were broken and the front steps to the porch began to sag. Everyone said it was an eyesore and ought to be torn down.

Anyway, a few years ago, some people got together and fixed up the house and turned it into the Maple Ridge Home for the Aged. They had the house painted on the outside, put in new windows, cemented the steps (but the porch still has big cracks in it), and turned one part of the house, 'way in back, into an infirmary. There's this one big room downstairs in the back, too, that looks like a dormitory.

The first time I walked up that path to the porch, even before I got inside, I felt weird. For one thing, there were all these old people sitting on the porch, rocking and rocking back and fortth. It was scary and strange, the way everyone stopped rocking when I walked up the steps and stared at me — all I wanted to do was turn around and run away. No wonder Mr. Pepper put up such a fight about coming here.

One old lady, the one closest to the steps, said, "Who're you looking for?" She was fat and kind of spilling over her seat from all sides; she had a loud, raspy voice and dark, glittering eyes.

"Mr. Pepper. Is he here?" Now wasn't that a silly question for me to ask? Where else would he be? But it shows you how peculiar I was feeling and I was still outside!

"Who does she want, Mabel?" a lady from the other end of the porch called out.

"Not you," the fat lady yelled back. "Busybody. Old Sarah Newton busybody," she said under her breath. "Has to know everybody's business. What do you want Mr. Pepper for?" Before I could answer, she went on, "Do I know you? I know everybody in town. Who's your father?"

"Chester Chadwick Cross." I didn't want to answer her, but I felt the way a butterfly must when it's pinned to a board, all fluttery and lost.

"Cross? Cross? What's your father do?"

"She doesn't have to tell you anything," a man sitting next to her said. He was as thin as she was fat. His eyes were so small I could hardly tell what color they were. I thought he was scrunching his eyes closed against the sunlight, but later I found out he just couldn't see very well. "You came to see Mr. Pepper, young lady? You just go on inside. You'll find him wandering around somewhere. They all do that when they first come, you know," he told me confidentially, practically leaning over the fat lady to give me the news. "But he'll get over it. They almost always do."

"She want me you say, Mabel?" the lady at the other end of the porch called out. "Tell her to come here. You come here, girlie. I want to talk to you."

"Never mind her," the old man said. "You go on inside now."

I was glad to get away from them. I could feel all their eyes boring into my back as I opened the screen door and then the big wooden door to the house. The first thing I saw was this big sweeping stairway almost directly in front of me, the kind that goes up half way and suddenly changes direction. I could just imagine one of the Bearley ladies in the olden days coming down to that first landing to look over the banister to see whoever was in the parlor — that's what they used to call the living room long ago — maybe just standing and waiting for someone to look up and see how beautifully she was dressed.

The reason I'm telling you this is because Mrs. Humphreys says you have to establish atmosphere. If you want to know, the atmosphere was oppressive. The room was dark — big and roomy, but dark.

The porch cut off a lot of light, and the shades were pulled down halfway on the one other big window at the side of the room to keep the sun out. There were more old people sitting in here. Some of them were sleeping, slumped down in their chairs. They made me think of sick, drooping birds. One old man was staring straight ahead, talking in a loud angry voice. Nobody was listening and it didn't make any difference because nothing he was saying made any sense at all. Beside him there was a woman wearing an apron which she was folding into tiny neat pleats, pressing each fold by running her fingers up and down it very carefully. Then she opened the pleats and started folding them all over again. She looked up just as I stared over at her. Her eyes were completely blank, like bare windows in an empty house.

One man was trying to read a newspaper. His hands were trembling and the paper was shaking so I couldn't understand how he could see what was on the page. But he kept at it, like a soldier who knows the battle is lost but goes on fighting anyway.

Two men were playing checkers in a corner of the room, paying absolutely no attention to anybody around them, just enjoying their game.

And at the other side of the room, an old lady was calmly getting undressed! Just then one of the nurses came running in. "No, no, no, Mrs. Parks. Not again. Put your dress back on. You don't want your daughter to see you like this, do you?"

"I don't like my daughter," Mrs. Parks said in a very pleasant voice. "I never did like her."

"Of course you like her. Mothers love their children," the nurse said, trying to slip the dress back on.

"Well I don't like mine," Mrs. Parks said, chattily. "She was a mean-spirited girl, and she's a mean-spirited woman."

One of the men playing checkers looked up, saw me, and grinned. He had china-blue eyes and a crinkly laughing expression even when he stopped grinning.

"Well! Aren't you a brave girl, getting past the rocking chair brigade out front," he said. "Can I help you, child?"

"I'm looking for Mr. Pepper," I explained.

"Oh. Our newcomer. He's probably out on the sun porch. Just go right through that doorway." He pointed to just beyond the stairway. "And along the corridor to the left."

I thanked him and made for the doorway. To tell you the truth, after what I'd just seen, what I really wanted to do was turn around and walk out. I felt I couldn't take another minute of this place. I just couldn't. I thought — if I don't get out of here, I'll die. I don't know how I forced myself through that doorway and into the corridor, but I had to. Because I had promised.

Just as I turned into the corridor, I ran smack into Mr. Pepper. "Opie! My, it is good to see you, my dear." He caught my hands in his and squeezed them.

He led me down the long corridor. They had built an annex to the house that couldn't be seen from the street. There were small bedrooms off on one side. I also caught a glimpse of a big dining room, with places set for the next meal. It looked surprisingly light and pleasant, in contrast to the dark living room. It was painted a light blue, with bright pictures on the wall, and flowers in the center of the table.

Mr. Pepper took me to a room at the very end of the corridor. And that was a surprise, too. Because it was an old-fashioned sun parlor, built in a circular pattern, with huge windows screened from top to bottom. There were plants on the floor, and on the radiator covers (I told you it was an old, old house), and even hanging from the ceiling. I found out later that Mr. Georgeby — he was one of the residents — was responsible for all the plants. The sun porch had lots of wicker furniture, too, with faded floral prints covering the backs and seats. The springs were coming through on a couple of the chairs, but at least the room had a quiet, open look. And there was nobody in it, except for Mr. Pepper and me.

Mr. Pepper was so glad to see me his eyes began to look tearful — some old people can get very emotional. So naturally I was simply stunned when the first words he said to me after we sat down were, "I don't ever want to see you here again, Opie. Not ever again."

"I thought you'd be glad to see me." I was really shocked.

"I'm delighted to see you. But I don't want you

to come here anymore. This is no place for a young girl. No, no. Don't interrupt me, Opie. This place is terrible. Terrible." He got up and started pacing around, the way a caged animal does, restless, around and around, stopping to glare at me, then going round and round again. "Did you see those people? Of course you did. Am I like that? Not yet. But I will be. I will be. They'll be shoving me into one of those rocking chairs one of these days."

"But I *promised,* Mr. Pepper," I tried to interrupt.

"Exactly," he said triumphantly, pointing his finger at me. "You got trapped by a promise. I release you from that promise. It was made out of pity. Well, young lady, I don't need pity. I need freedom. I need to live in my own house and be my own man. That's what I need."

"You need to calm down, Pepper," a voice said from the doorway. It was the man with the china-blue eyes. "Pay no attention, my dear," he told me. "He's in shock. We all go through it, one way or another." He came and sat beside me, and patted my hand.

"She came to see me, Smithers, not you," Mr. Pepper said.

"Well, from the way you were talking to her, she may never come back."

"Good," Mr. Pepper snapped.

"No, it isn't. It isn't good at all. That's our problem. We need to have young people around us." He leaned over and talked to me in a kind of confidential way. "Right now, my dear . . . what's your name? Opie? Right now, Opie, you see us like grapes in a cluster. You can't tell one of us from the other. But you keep coming back, young lady, and after a while, you'll sort us out. Can you understand?"

I nodded. I really could see what he was getting at, because I remember how it was the first time I walked into Northview Junior High. I got that same overwhelmed feeling (well maybe not exactly, but it was a sort of sinking sensation, scared), because I didn't know if I was going to like my teachers or hate them. But after a while, you get to know who's who, like Mr. Johns who swears by the textbook like it's holy script, and Mrs. Porter, who's been there forever and she knows who you are because she had your older sister and maybe even your mother in her class, and old Miss Fuss-pot in Home Room, Miss Fussy Phillips with her "study hall is for studying, Penelope!"

One thing I knew right away. I wouldn't have any trouble picking Mr. Smithers out of the group. I think he's the kind of person that always got noticed right away, wherever he was.

I started to tell him that I really did understand, but before I could open my mouth, a man came rushing in. He was a short man, and dark — dark hair, dark eyes, dark mustache, and ears that stood away from his head. He looked like a worried rabbit, something like the White Rabbit in *Alice in Wonderland* — the one that's always screaming, "I'm late! I'm late!" Honestly, when he started to talk that's what I half expected him to say.

What he did say was, "Have you seen Mrs. Longwood?"

Smithers and Mr. Pepper both shook their heads.

"Gone again, Mr. Ver Lees?"

"Gone again," Mr. Ver Lees said unhappily.

"Here's Opie," Mr. Smithers told him. "She's got good strong young feet. Send her chasing after Mrs. Longwood."

"Excellent. Excellent. Quick, Opie. She'll be heading north on Central. She always heads north. Hurry. Mrs. Longwood walks very fast."

"I don't even know who she is," I started to protest, but Mr. Ver Lees was holding my arm and sort of pushing me out.

"You can't miss her. She's tall, has gray hair pulled back in a tight bun, walks with a good stride, arms swinging. Has an identity tag on her right wrist."

"Don't worry, Opie," Mr. Smithers said cheerfully. "I'll be walking behind you . . . way behind you, I'm afraid." He held up a cane, which I hadn't noticed before when I was so busy with Mr. Pepper.

"But suppose she won't come back with me," I wailed. "How will I get her to come back?"

"Just take her by the hand," Mr. Ver Lees said impatiently.

We were out on the porch now. Everybody began to babble at once. "Mr. Ver Lees. Mr. Ver Lees." I found out later that Mr. Ver Lees is the director of Maple Ridge, which explains the way he looks. I could hear his name over and over as I went down the steps, ran along the walk, and started to race north along Central, looking for a tall, fast-moving old lady.

At first I didn't see anybody — well, you know what I mean. There were some kids on skateboards, and a couple on bikes, and a lady walking her dog. Then I did catch sight of Mrs. Longwood, and she really was swinging right along, as if she had some-place to go and not much time to get there. I tell you, by the time I caught up with her, I was gasping for breath.

"Mrs. Longwood," I yelled, before I reached her.

She didn't turn around or pay any attention at all. "Mrs. Longwood."

Two little kids began yelling, too. "Hey, Mrs. Longwood. Somebody wants you. Yoo-hoo, Mrs. Longwood."

Talk about single-minded determination. If I tell you that Maple Ridge is down near 36th Street, and she was only a few blocks from the Broad Ripple Canal when I caught up to her . . . I mean, we could have entered her in the Olympics!

When I came up alongside of her, I just grabbed her hand. "Wait a minute, Mrs. Longwood," I pleaded. "I have to catch my breath."

She stopped and looked at me. "Do I know you?" she asked. She had a light, feathery kind of voice which didn't seem to go with the rest of her — the tallness, the muscular gait, the strong-featured face — but it was pleasing to listen to.

"I'm Opie Cross. Listen, Mrs. Longwood." I was still holding her hand, and now I began to pull at her a little. "Mr. Ver Lees is very upset. He was looking for you."

"Why did he send you?" I swear Mrs. Longwood sounded very disappointed. "They usually send a police car after me. They always think I'm going to get lost. Me! I was born right over on Delaware Street. I was married there. Lost my husband there. Know this town like I know the palm of my hand."

All the time she was keeping up this stream of conversation (only it was more like a monologue. She didn't seem to need anybody at the other end of it except to listen, maybe), she just turned around and started walking back with me.

"I really will have to complain to Mr. Ver Lees." She was still going on. "I *always* get back to Maple Ridge in a police car. What will they think? There's no style coming back this way."

"You never came back with me before." I didn't think that was any big deal, but it was all I could think of right off the bat.

She stopped and really looked at me now. "That's true, isn't it? Did all those old biddies on the porch see you?" I nodded. "And try to talk to you?" I nodded again. She began to giggle. She sounded the way Marvin does when he's being silly. It was queer, coming from her, and made me a little nervous. "Well, what are we waiting for?" she asked. She got a tight grip on my hand and we went tearing back down Central.

Just before we reached Maple Ridge, we met Mr. Smithers.

"Did you get to see the ducks, Madeline?" he asked cheerfully.

"No ducks. I never got to the Canal. This is Opie. Where did she come from?"

"She's one of the new volunteers," Mr. Smithers replied.

"No, I'm not," I started to say, but Mrs. Longwood was pulling me right along, up the walk, and on to the porch. Mr. Ver Lees came out the front door just as we arrived.

"I'm disappointed in you, Madeline," he said sadly. "You promised me you wouldn't go running off again."

She was very good at changing the subject. "You didn't tell me we had a new volunteer."

Mr. Ver Lees' eyes lit up. "You've volunteered? That's marvelous."

That's where I made my big mistake. Instead of trying to find a nice way out, I just should have said right out that one, I wasn't a volunteer, two, I didn't want to be a volunteer, and three, if I decided to be a volunteer for anything, it wouldn't be at Maple Ridge. I couldn't just come right out and say I found the atmosphere too depressing — all those old people rocking on the porch — or tell them about the hollow feeling I got in the pit of my stomach when I walked inside the Home. So I just said instead, "I'm still in school," thinking that would take care of it.

"Oh, we wouldn't expect you to help out on school days, Opie. Unless, of course, you have some free time?"

"Well, I have a short day on Wednesdays." That kind of popped out before I knew what I was saying.

"Wednesdays. Wonderful. And Saturday afternoons? Or mornings, if you prefer," he added quickly. "And of course, school will be out soon. You'll like the other volunteers, Opie. Lovely girls. Very dedicated. Have you spoken to Mrs. Orrmont yet? She's head of the Maple Ridge Guild. You'll want to get in touch with her. She'll tell you what our girls do to help. Wonderful thing you girls are doing for us. Wonderful!"

He looked around, counting heads, I guess, and then disappeared inside.

Mr. Smithers was up on the porch, grinning at me.

"You don't know what hit you, do you? That's our Mr. Ver Lees. I've seen him get money for the Home the same way. I don't know where we would be without him."

"But I never volunteered," I said, still in shock. "All I did was come see Mr. Pepper."

Mr. Smithers leaned forward. He wasn't smiling

now, just looking at me very earnestly. "We need you, my dear. We really very desperately need you."

What could I say? What would you have said?

So I went back inside, dragging my feet — I admit it — and went looking for Mrs. Orrmont.

Opie involved, that's what I was. The only trouble with getting involved like this is that one thing always kind of leads to another, and that's how I got all mixed up with worrying about Mrs. Sherman, and it was Mrs. Sherman and the Rebellion I was going to tell you about before. Only first I've been still laying the foundation, just the way Mrs. Humphreys told us to. It's easy for Mrs. Humphreys to say, but let me tell you, laying foundations is really very hard work.

Chapter Four

I couldn't believe that a whole month had gone by since I went in to see Mrs. Orrmont. I can still remember how weird I felt when I went into her tiny cubbyhole of an office, right off the nurses' station. It was a kind of mixed-up sensation, a little like that time in third grade when I had to see the principal after I punched Gary Trivett in the nose in the schoolyard.

Mrs. Orrmont is a short lady who looks tall when she's sitting down. When she stands up, you feel surprised that there isn't more of her. She has this way of staring at your lips when you talk as if she might miss something important if she looked away for a minute. It made me very nervous till I got used to it.

I explained that I wanted to volunteer to work at Maple Ridge but first would she tell me what did a volunteer do?

"Oh, our candy-stripers do just about everything," she told me. "They help the residents walk up and down the corridor, take them back and forth to the dining room, or out on the porch. They take some of the residents down to the basement, to the arts-and-crafts room down there. Play records. Read. Write letters for them. Visit." She leaned back in her chair. She had a big paper clip in her hands which she kept turning around in her fingers. That's another thing I noticed about Mrs. Orrmont. She was always fidgeting with something while she talked — straightening papers on her desk, or playing with a pencil or a paper clip, or drawing little boxes on a scratch pad and then filling them in. "But the most important thing of all, Opie, is just plain listening. They want to talk. They desperately need to talk."

"Don't they talk to each other?" I asked.

"Of course. But it's talking to someone from the outside world that stimulates them. And it's talking to someone young. You can't imagine what it means to them, to see young faces around them."

That didn't sound hard, I mean, what a volunteer had to do. What was hard was getting used to Maple Ridge. At first I spent only about an hour there on Wednesdays, and another hour on Saturday mornings. Then, when school was out, Mrs. Orrmont asked me to come in for two hours a day four times a week.

"That strikes me as being pretty excessive," my Mom said when I told her and my Dad what I was going to do. To tell you the truth, my Mom was down on the whole idea. "I think two hours a *week* is more than enough in that awful place."

"I think Mom's right," Lissie said, which surprised me because usually she doesn't take much interest in what I do. Right now the big thing in Lissie's life — aside from planning what she's going to do at Indiana University in the fall — is dating.

My Dad tells me that Lissie and I will be good friends someday when we're older, which is hard to believe. All I can say is right now, we argue an awful lot because Lissie has this way of acting like she's the queen bee and I'm one of her little drones.

"Two hours a day is too much to ask of a volunteer," Lissie went on.

My Dad disagreed. "Opie's out at the pool three afternoons a week." I forgot to mention I have this part-time job as a lifeguard at the Center. My folks don't think lying around all summer doing nothing is a good idea. "She gets plenty of air and sunshine. As long as she wants to help out . . ." He looked at me, sort of leaving it for me to finish his thought.

"It's not too bad," I said. "I'm kind of used to it now. Besides, when you get to know them, the way I have this past month, you have a whole different feeling about it all."

It's true. Look at old Mr. Handy. He's sweet as pie, even though he does steal the silverware. The first time I saw him putting the silverware in his pocket, I ran into Mrs. Orrmont's office and yelled, "There's an old man in there who's putting the silverware in his pocket!"

Mrs. Orrmont just shrugged and said, "That's all right, Opie. That's Mr. Handy. Later on, just go into his room and ask if you can borrow the silverware. He'll give it back."

"But why do you let him do that?" I asked, and she just looked at me and said, "Why not, Opie? He's not hurting anybody. Mr. Handy is gentle as a lamb. He's just a mild kleptomaniac, that's all. You just be nice to him."

That really scared me — I never met a kleptomaniac before — and later, when they told me to go and get the silverware, I was afraid to go but I did. I just knocked on his door and went in, and said kind of fast and nervous, "Uh, Mr. Handy, could I borrow some silverware from you? We're kind of short in the kitchen."

And this old gentleman — he has the softest brown eyes, big and round, and a long, mournful face that reminds me of a basset hound we used to have — got up from his chair and he said, "Why bless you, child, it would be my great pleasure." And he went and got all the silverware out of his drawer and dumped it on the tray I had brought with me. "Now you must come to me whenever you need table service," he told me with a very serious expression, "because I always have enough and to spare."

And then there's Mrs. Lee. At first I thought she was strange. She never would sit with anybody else. In the living room, she's always 'way off at the end of the room, right near the door that leads to the corridor. Out on the porch, there's a part of it that takes a small turn around the building. There's just enough room for one chair there. That's where I always walk with her. She doesn't see too well, but if that bothers her, she sure never complains about it. She doesn't complain about anything, and that's a fact. Like they have these hard metal chairs on the porch. Mrs. Lee's metal chair is a rocker, but I swear I didn't know how she could sit on it hour after hour. So one day I brought a pillow. Big deal, you know? It wasn't even a *new* pillow. But she pulled my face down and kissed me on both cheeks. You'd have thought I gave her the keys to the Taj Mahal or something.

She is an absolute lamb. The other day I went past her, rocking as usual in the far end of the living room all by herself. I said, "Hi, Mrs. Lee. You look nice and comfortable."

She called me closer, peering up at me. Then she took my hand in hers — her hands were so warm — and she said, "When I was a little baby, Opie, my mother held me in her arms and she rocked me. And she rocked me when I was a little girl when I was sad or hurt or scared. And then I grew up and had children of my own, and my own rocker for their quiet times and their sad times and their hurting times. And now here I am, all alone with my rocker, and nothing to rock but my memories."

Well I got this great big lump in my throat. I asked her, "Can I come to you when I have sad times, and you can be my grandmother?"

Two tears rolled down her face, and she whispered, with her voice kind of hoarse the way it gets when you're trying to keep from crying, "You come whenever you like, child. But I hope life doesn't hold too many sad times for you, my dear."

She really got to me, and I walked away with tears in my own eyes and I didn't care if anybody saw me or not. I found out from Mrs. Orrmont that Mrs. Lee is another one who never gets any visitors. Nobody ever comes to see her.

"Maybe her family is scattered. Or they live too

far away to come and see her. Like Edith Pepper," my Mom reminded me when we were sitting and eating supper that night. My Mom is always ready with some kind of reasonable explanation. But I don't think that's the whole story. I believe it's more what Mr. Smithers says. "Old people . . . old parents," Mr. Smithers told me once, "are in the way, especially if they're any kind of physical or financial problem to their children. Some of us need almost as much attention as newborn babies. The problem is, Opie," he smiled at me but he was feeling depressed — they all get depressed every once in a while, even the ones like Mr. Smithers who puts on such a happy face most of the time — "we're not cuddly and lovable. We're at the wrong end of the stick."

"I think Opie spends too much time at Maple Ridge," my Mom told my Dad. "I really do."

"Anyway," Lissie added suddenly, "I can't see why they're your problem. If their own children don't care, why should you?"

"It's my problem because I'm involved in it," I snapped back at her, "and maybe that's what you ought to be, instead of going out with drips like Harold and Woody and George."

My Mom looked at me and she said, in a real worried voice, "Aren't you taking all of this too much to heart, Opie?"

"No. I'm not. I really love old Mrs. Lee. And Mr. Smithers. And some of the others, too."

"Oh, you love everybody there," Lissie said, bored. She looked at her watch, and gasped. "Can I please be excused?" We've been saying that since we were old enough to talk and Lissie just says it out of habit because she was up out of her chair and running upstairs before the words were out of her mouth.

But I have to tell you that what Lissie said is absolutely not true. I don't love them all. There are some people at Maple Ridge I just can't stand. You take fat old Mabel Yore — she's the lady who gave me the third degree when I walked up on the porch the very first time I set foot at Maple Ridge. I never talk to her if I can help it. It's not because she's old and fat and ugly. It's because she gives off these bad vibrations, like she's all twisted inside with meanness. And I don't like her cronies, either. Sarah Newton and Emma Fisher — I bet they'd have sat around the guillotine knitting and cackling when the heads rolled during the French Revolution. But Mabel Yore is the worst of the lot. If she was skinny, she'd be perfect as the Wicked Witch of the West.

I wouldn't like Mabel Yore or Sarah Newton or Emma Fisher if they were my own age, like a lot of people in school I could mention but I won't.

The reason I'm telling you all this is because of Mrs. Humphreys. We had to write character sketches last month and I got mine back, looking as if it was dripping with blood. See, Mrs. Humphreys makes comments all over your paper in red ink. She's got this marvelous handwriting — all her letters look like they're on parade and just passing the reviewing stand, tall and straight with their backs starched. Well, those red words were marching up, down, and across all four sheets of my sketch. Right on top, Mrs. Humphreys wrote, "I do not *see* your characters, Opie! Make me SEE them!"

So I certainly hope you see the people at Maple Ridge because I'd hate to have to start all over again.

Anyway, getting back to the people I like and the people I don't like at Maple Ridge. I wasn't really sure that I even liked Mrs. Sherman at first. She's a tiny thing, all silvery. Silver hair and silver eyebrows and silver lashes and silver glasses. And gray eyes that have a silver look to them. Lissie says that's impossible, nobody has silver eyes, but that's the way they look to me.

I thought she was kind of peppery, the way she

talked to me at first. And *proud?* Talking to her sometimes was like trying to walk on eggshells without cracking them.

The first time I saw her, she was walking down that long corridor, more like wandering, kind of, and she had such a lost sad look, my heart went out to her, like my Mom always says. So I went up to her and said, "Wouldn't you like to come to the arts-and-crafts room? I'll bring you downstairs if you like."

She stopped and glared at me. "Busywork to keep me out of mischief? I used to give my children crayons and coloring books. Do they have any coloring books down there?"

"No, honestly," I told her, thinking to myself all the while, oh great, she's one of the cranky ones. "Some of the things they're making are really nice. Mrs. Paul is painting the prettiest flowers and Mr. Spann is making a lovely ashtray."

"Mrs. Paul couldn't paint the side of a barn if somebody held the brush for her," she answered. "And to call those sickening globs of clay ashtrays requires either charity or blindness."

"Now, dear," I said in that soothing voice I heard some of the nurses use.

Well you should have seen the way she turned on me. And her voice got real sharp. "I am not your dear. I have a name, young lady. A perfectly good name. I'm Mrs. Sherman. And don't you ever use that tone of voice to me again!" She went on, almost as if she was talking to herself, very crossly, "I don't know why people think that if you're old, you have to be treated like a small child. A small backward child. Or a congenital idiot. I'm not senile. My mind is as clear and sharp as yours, maybe sharper. And I could teach you a thing or two, young woman. So don't you come around patronizing me!"

And with that off her chest, she trotted back down the corridor, only she didn't look lost and sad anymore, only good and mad.

She really gave me something to think about, because after that I found myself listening to the way the volunteers and the regular help and even the visitors talked to the old people, and Mrs. Sherman was right. I could hear how false and patient they sounded, and — Mrs. Sherman used the exact word to describe it — patronizing. Everybody kind of talks down to the residents, especially the volunteers like me. I suppose we feel we're doing them a big favor just by being there, and of course in a way we are. But there really is something wrong about that attitude. I mean, I would just hate it if anybody used that voice on me.

The next time I saw Mrs. Sherman, I purposely went into her room. Because that's what I was doing that day, going from room to room, visiting. Funny, you don't have to stay long, only about ten minutes, but the way the residents perk up is terrific. Mrs. Sherman had the door to her room open, and she was sitting and reading a magazine. A French magazine! *Le Monde,* I think it was called. I suppose I looked stunned. I don't know why — after all, French is a perfectly reasonable language after you get used to it — and of course Mrs. Sherman noticed how surprised I was and right off the bat she said, "You're doing it again, aren't you?" She didn't get mad this time, just sighed.

"This modern world," she said. "Men on the moon, space satellites, robots on Mars shooting film, a pacemaker here," she pointed at her chest, "but no idea at all about people. It's strange," she went on. "Scientists have been so busy learning how to keep us alive longer. But the problem is, they haven't learned what to do with us. So we end up in places like Maple Ridge. Well," she added philosophically, "at least it isn't called Happy Vale."

"*Happy* Vale?" I echoed.

"There's a place out in California I almost went to called Happy Vale. Ridiculous name! There's nothing happy about a home for the aged. How could there be? Euphemisms!" She just went right on talking, and I suddenly realized that Mrs. Sherman was really starved for conversation. "Do you know what a euphemism is?"

Well, honestly! I'm not dumb, you know. I might not use big words and all but that doesn't mean I don't know them.

"Euphemism. Substituting a 'nice' word for something that sounds kind of grim, like saying 'passed away' instead of 'died.' " As soon as I said that, I got red in the face. One thing you never want to do is talk about dying to an old person.

She laughed at me. "Now, Opie, I'm not going to faint. One of the hazards of living is dying. That's something scientists are never going to change." Her eyes were full of mischief. I personally didn't see how she could joke about it.

Later, at supper, when I was telling Mom and Dad about Mrs. Sherman, Lissie said, "She sounds dreadful."

"She is not. She's . . ." I had to stop and think. I was going to say nice, but what kind of a word is that? Nice. It's a nice day. That's a nice blouse. This is a nice place. It's no kind of word at all.

"Interesting?" my Mom suggested.

My Dad didn't say anything, just chewed on the stem of his pipe and waited for me to sort it out in my mind.

". . . a first-class human being," I finished. "I listen to Mrs. Sherman, and I don't think about her as being an old lady in a Home. I think about her the way I think about Grandma . . ."

"What is it, Opie?" my Dad wanted to know when my voice kind of trailed away.

"Well, Mrs. Sherman says we live in a labeled society. She says when you stick a label on a group of people they aren't individuals anymore. She's a quote senior citizen and I'm a quote teen-ager — like we've been sorted out and dumped into baskets marked potatoes, or onions. Mrs. Sherman says she isn't a senior citizen, she is an individual, a *person,* who has lived a long time and so she is an old lady. But she is her *own* old lady . . . Daddy, do you know what I mean?"

"Well, what difference does it make?" Lissie asked. She hates these kinds of discussions. See, Lissie is more into physical things, like being a cheerleader at the football games, and baton twirling. She's going to study phys. ed. down at I.U. because she wants to be a gym teacher.

My Dad is okay, though. You can really talk to

him. Now he got up from the table, came by my chair and kissed me on top of my head. Daddy doesn't do that very much anymore, now that Lissie and I are adults, well, almost. It gave me a good feeling.

"I like your Mrs. Sherman," he said. "She's giving you some valuable insights."

"I guess I'm really involved," I told him.

"That's the name of the game, Opie," he said, and left the room.

Chapter Five

"You know what?" I said the next evening, at the supper table. "I think Mr. Pepper is sweet on Mrs. Sherman."

My Mom put her fork down and stared at me. "Simon *Pepper?*"

Have you ever noticed how people do that, repeat a name, I mean, with the emphasis on the last name, when they can't believe something you've just said? What other Peppers do we know?

Lissie wrinkled her nose. "I think that's disgusting!" she said.

"You don't even know Mrs. Sherman . . ."

"And I don't want to. It's absolutely disgusting."

"Simon Pepper, of all people," my Mom said slowly.

"Why of all people?" my Dad broke in. "Don't you think Simon has a right to some emotions?"

"At his age?"

"What has age got to do with it?" my Dad asked reasonably.

My Mom looked at my father and then looked away. Her face got kind of pink. "Don't be ridiculous, Chet. Simon Pepper is seventy-five years old."

"Is that the cutoff period for a little affection or companionship?"

"There are times I simply don't understand you, Chet."

"What's wrong with Mr. Pepper liking Mrs. Sherman?" I wondered. "It's making living at Maple Ridge so much easier for them both. You don't know what it's like, Mom . . . ."

"Thank God for that!"

". . . but if you had to live there . . ."

She shuddered.

". . . you'd understand how they feel. Could we ask Mrs. Sherman over next time Mr. Pepper comes for dinner?"

My Dad didn't say a word, just waited, biting on the stem of his pipe.

"Not next time, no, Opie." My Mom carefully avoided looking over at my Dad.

"Well, when?"

"Don't push me," she snapped. "Some time. Later on." She threw her napkin down on the table. "It seems to me, Penelope," she said coldly, "that you'd be better off doing some serious reading instead of tearing off to Maple Ridge all the time. If you expect to be any kind of English teacher at all!"

"What Opie is doing is fine," my Dad defended me. "She's being exposed to one aspect of social work. It's invaluable experience."

"Hey!" I objected. "Whatever happened to good old-fashioned fun? Is everybody forgetting that I'm only fourteen? Why are you guys after me all the time?"

"Well! I certainly don't want to be accused of putting any pressure on you, Opie," my Dad said, and now his voice was dripping icicles, too.

My Mom got up and started to clear the dishes from the table. "Am I going to have to do this all by myself?" she demanded.

Lissie and I got up and got busy. When my mother gets that certain tone of voice, it's easier to help than to argue, believe me. My Dad walked out and we heard the door to the den slam.

"I wish I'd never heard of Maple Ridge," my Mom muttered under her breath. Lissie looked daggers at me. "There goes my date with Grover," she hissed when my Mom was at the sink. "You know she won't let me date Grover when she's mad."

Lissie thinks Grover is a Greek god or something because he's going to be a junior in college next semester. Grover is what my Dad calls a computer bank for trivia. When he's waiting for Lissie — one thing you have to know about Lissie is that she wouldn't dream of being on time for anything — he'll say things to my Dad like, "Did you know that on this date in 1859 the first intercollegiate baseball game was played in Pittsfield, Massachusetts?" My Dad is very courteous. He'll answer, "Is that a fact, Grover," and rattle his paper. Then Grover, after waiting a minute, always adds some big punch line, like "Amherst beat Williams then, sixty-six to thirty-two."

"Thank you, Grover." Then Dad will give me this significant nod of the head which means will I *please* go upstairs and build a fire under Lissie.

Every time Lissie and Grover walk out of the front door, my Dad says, "What those two find to talk about I can't imagine. It makes the mind boggle."

Anyway, getting back to Mrs. Sherman (Mrs. Humphreys says I must learn to stick to my theme but I can't help the way my mind works), I was satisfied for the time being. I figured sooner or later my Mom would give in. She really likes Mr. Pepper.

Next morning, when I went over to Maple Ridge, Mr. Pepper met me at the door. I thought it was because he wanted to find out if my Mom agreed to invite Mrs. Sherman to our house. I forgot to tell you it was Mr. Pepper who asked me to ask my Mom. He wanted Mrs. Sherman to have a chance to eat a home-cooked meal around a family table. I think that's the saddest thing. To long to be with a family at the dinner table. But he didn't even mention it. He looked worried.

"Opie," he said. "Could you go see Mrs. Sherman?"

"Is she sick?" That's the first thing you think of when you're around old people, I guess. I got a kind of sinking sensation. Not Mrs. Sherman, I thought. Please, not Mrs. Sherman.

"Not sick, Opie. Upset. She's been crying. But she won't tell me why. She won't tell anybody why."

Well, I went running off to Mrs. Sherman's room. I knocked on the door and without waiting for an answer I walked right in. Mrs. Sherman had her head turned away. She made some quick swipes at her eyes with her handkerchief and blew her nose and pretended she was coming down with a cold, but I knew better. Mr. Pepper was right. Mrs. Sherman had been crying.

Mr. Pepper was right about another thing. Mrs. Sherman wouldn't talk about it. Not at first, anyway. But I'm a lot like my father. I can be stubborn and persistent when I want to get at the heart of a matter, so I finally broke her down and got the whole story.

It seems Mrs. Sherman had bought this cemetery plot and had paid for it in advance, and then she had bought a headstone for it and paid for that in advance, too. The only thing was, the company went out of business and they never did put up the headstone, and now Mrs. Sherman didn't have any money left to buy another one.

I guess if I hadn't become used to the way Mrs. Sherman thinks I would have thought the whole thing was pretty gruesome. But I could see how she felt about it. It was something very personal.

Anyway, I said something about how it was a rotten shame, which is the kind of thing you say automatically, but it really was, cheating somebody on a *gravestone* . . . I mean, that's practically sacrilegious! So without thinking I said something about how maybe she could borrow the money from Mr. Pepper or we could take up a collection, thinking it would calm her down, and I thought she would bite my head off.

"Charity!" she said, looking at me as if I had turned into Godzilla the monster. And she got up from the bed and sat down in a chair near the window and began to crochet like mad.

"Well, it's not a dirty word you know," I said, sort of mad myself. After all, it's right there in the Bible *...and now abideth faith, hope, charity, these three; but the greatest of these is charity.*

"It is a word that should be stricken from the English language." Mrs. Sherman's voice was icy. "Thank you for dropping by but I think Id like to be alone now, Opie."

I started to go out of the room but I felt awful. I just couldn't leave her like that, sitting there so helpless and defeated. So I just came closer and asked her what she was making. She sighed.

"What I'm making is as out of this world as I am, Opie. I'm making an antimacassar." She saw the expression on my face and laughed. "You haven't the foggiest idea what an antimacassar is, poor child. It's a doily. Years ago, people used to put antimacassars on the backs of chairs and sofas and along the arms to keep the upholstery from getting soil spots. I don't know why I still make them. They're about as useful now as the one-horse shay. I've got piles of them in that drawer over there." She looked down at the crocheting needle and the yarn wrapped around her finger. "I guess old habits die hard. It's not easy to sit with your hands idle when they've been busy for a lifetime."

I watched her for a few minutes. It looked easy and sort of fun. "Will you teach me how to crochet?" I could tell that pleased her.

She gave me a needle and some yarn and showed me what she called a few basic simple stitches. Simple!

I was practicing at home that evening when Lissie came by. "What in the world are you doing?" she asked me, though it was plain as day what I was doing ... getting everything all fouled up. It looked so effortless when Mrs. Sherman's fingers were flying. And the designs she makes. I mean, they are just unbelievable. "Don't tell me," Lissie said before I could answer. "It's probably something your precious Mrs. Sherman's gotten you into."

Just then my Mom came in to turn on the TV and I had this idea. "Mom, would you like to buy some antimacassars?"

Her mouth dropped open. "Antima*cass*ars? Whatever for?"

"Do you know anybody who would?"

"Whatever for?" she asked again.

"That's what I figured," I said gloomily. I put the crocheting aside. I wasn't getting anywhere with it anyhow, so I just sat and looked at TV and brooded. My mind wasn't really on TV and then this commercial came on. Talk about subliminal advertising!

I wasn't even paying attention; it was something about Block's or Ayres having a sale on sheets and pillowcases and bedspreads . . . like, who cared? And that's when it hit me.

I got up and ran to the den. It's not actually a den at all, but that's what my Mom likes to call it. It's this little room that my Dad uses because he brings home a lot of paperwork. I knocked on the door and my Dad called out impatiently, "Whoever it is, go away. I'm busy."

"Daddy, I've got to talk to you," I said and I opened the door. His brows came together and he had this glazed look he gets when he's concentrating heavily, but I just plunged right in because I needed his help. "I need your help desperately."

"Can it wait?" he asked hopefully.

"Daddy, how do you go about making up a raffle?"

He was getting ready to explode but then he saw how serious I was, so he took one of his deep breaths, settled back, and, after he listened, he gave me the information that I wanted.

The next thing, of course, was to get back to Mrs. Sherman, which is what I did the very next morning. I just burst in on her and said, "Mrs. Sherman. I've got this super idea and please don't say no until you've heard the whole plan. You know those antimacassars?

They're really beautiful handwork. And people will pay all kinds of fancy prices for handwork. Especially if it's something that is useful as well as decorative."

"Opie, no one will buy . . ."

I didn't let her finish, because I knew what she was going to say but she didn't know what I had in mind. So I just steamrollered right over her objections.

"Mrs. Sherman. Listen. If you could sew those antimacassars together, we could sell them as a hand-made bedspread."

"Sell it how?"

The idea was so clear in my own head I was surprised she couldn't see it too.

"A raffle!"

"I don't know anything about raffles, Opie."

"You don't have to," I said eagerly. "I talked the whole thing over with my Dad and he told me how to go about it. He's going to have the tickets printed. And we'll sell them, and somebody will get a treasure. And you'll get enough money to buy a new headstone. And don't tell me *that's* charity," I went on, "because my very own mother said she would give her eyeteeth for a handmade bedspread. She said handmade bed-spreads are collectors' items. Listen, Mrs. Sherman, my Mom practically turns green with envy whenever she takes a look at Mrs. Goldsmith's bedspread. Mrs.

Goldsmith is Marvin's mother." Mrs. Sherman nodded. She knew who Marvin was because I told her how I had to baby-sit with him when the Goldsmiths go out. "Mrs. Goldsmith's grandmother made it. Mrs. Goldsmith calls it her 'heirloom' spread."

"Does your grandmother crochet?" Mrs. Sherman asked. I had to laugh. My grandmother is great at whipping out angry letters to the editor of the *Star,* or snapping at *Time* Magazine for some of their articles, but sitting down with a needle and yarn? Forget it!

"So will you sew the antimacassars together?"

"Certainly not," Mrs. Sherman replied calmly. She grinned at my expression. "But I will crochet them together."

She went to the dresser and opened a drawer.

"Help me put these on the bed, Opie. I want to pick out the proper patterns."

We were doing that when there was a knock on the door. Mr. Pepper stuck his head in.

"Is everything all right?" he asked. His eyes opened wide when he saw the bed. "What's going on?"

"Simon," Mrs. Sherman said cheerfully. "Come in. Help me sort these out, will you?"

When I left, they were busy arranging the antimacassars according to the different designs. I thought they wouldn't even notice me leaving. But just as I was about to close the door, Mrs. Sherman looked up and said, "Leave the door open, Opie. We don't want tongues wagging any more than necessary."

Would you believe that? In this day and age? And with them so old and all?

Just the same, I noticed that everybody walking by Mrs. Sherman's room — and I don't mean only the residents, but everybody, the nurses and the volunteers and the visitors — all looked in that open door as they walked by.

Chapter Six

You know how sometimes you hear people talking and you don't pay any attention because you're not very interested, and then you hear your name and your ears kind of perk up? I wasn't planning on eavesdropping or anything, but I was coming down the steps and my Mom and Dad were in the living room deep in conversation. I could hear them, a sort of swell of words, more like murmurs, bzzz, bzzz, bzzz, and then my name flying up in the air . . . Opie. So I came down a few more steps and sat down. They couldn't see me, but I could hear them clearly.

"I don't see what the problem is," my Dad was saying.

"I'm telling you that Opie has changed. And I'm not sure I like what's happening."

"I'll agree with part of that," my Dad replied, "if by changing you mean that our daughter is growing up. Maturing. She's on her way to becoming a responsible adult."

"At fourteen? She has plenty of time to become a responsible adult, for heaven's sake."

"I still don't see what the problem is," my Dad repeated patiently.

"She spends entirely too much time with old people. It's just not natural . . ."

"That's not it at all," my Dad interrupted. "You know how Opie is. When she starts something, she sees it through. I happen to think that's an admirable trait . . ."

I liked that, especially the admirable part, though I guess you really can't take credit for something that's part of your nature.

My Mom wasn't finished. "I just don't understand you at times, Chet. Opie is at the age when she should be thinking about her social life, having a good time. Don't you remember how Lissie was at this age? You wouldn't have found Lissie worrying over things like Mrs. Sherman and her gravestone . . ."

"Which came to a very satisfactory conclusion," my Dad reminded her.

I nodded in agreement. It certainly did. Even my Mom bought raffle tickets — a whole book of them, as a matter of fact. And all her friends practically fought over them. The women desperately wanted that bedspread because it was what my Mom called a 'prestige item.' I was sorry my Mom didn't get to win it. Mrs. Rice did — she lives over on the next block — she bought five books! It's just as well she got it, I guess, because her children are grown and married, and she doesn't have any pets, and her husband wouldn't dare lie down on the bed when it's made so you know nothing will ever happen to that bedspread. She was really sweet after she won it (we held the prize-giving right at Maple Ridge). Mrs. Rice went up to Mrs. Sherman and kissed her and said, "I will treasure this all my days, and I will think of you and your golden hands every time I look at it."

The very next day, my Dad and I drove Mrs. Sherman over to that monument place. I thought I'd die, all those headstones just standing around waiting. But Mrs. Sherman was happy as a lark. It was just a small stone, more like a marker than anything, but Mrs. Sherman acted like somebody had just given her the keys to the kingdom or something.

She paid for it "with my own money" she told the monument man, and she wanted it put up right away on her plot so she could go out and see for herself that it was there.

And early this morning, while Mom went to church, my Dad and I picked up Mrs. Sherman and Mr. Pepper at Maple Ridge and drove them out to the cemetery. Mrs. Sherman showed us where her plot is, and there was the marker with her name on it, with the date she was born and a blank space for you know what. When I looked at that blank space, just waiting to be filled in, I got this awful creepy feeling. I thought Mrs. Sherman and Mr. Pepper must have that feeling, too. But they didn't. Mrs. Sherman ran her hand over that stone, kind of loving-like, and she said to Mr. Pepper, "Isn't this rose color handsome, Simon?"

"Beautiful, Serena," he said. "Just beautiful." I guess I will never truly understand some people because personally I couldn't say a word, what with being in the cemetery and all.

Mrs. Sherman turned to my Dad and sighed, like you do when something is over with that's been on your mind for a long time, and she said, "I have never liked loose ends, Mr. Cross."

My Dad put his arm around her and said of course and that he understood. He can be so nice!

Before we left, Mrs. Sherman lifted her face up and said, "What a lovely breeze. So refreshing. How tranquil one can be here at last. Do you feel it, Simon?"

"I'm not ready to be that tranquil, Serena," Mr. Pepper protested.

Mrs. Sherman patted the headstone. "Nor am I —
yet. But there have been times when I was ready."

Mr. Pepper nodded grimly. "I was ready, the first
time I set foot in Maple Ridge." His expression soft-
ened. "Until I met you, Serena."

They looked at each other across the headstone so
lovingly that Dad took my arm and walked me away.

"I'm so glad they found each other," I blurted out.

"You *are* growing up," my Dad said. "You're quite
a girl, Opie."

But judging from the way their conversation was
going in the living room right now, I could tell my
parents weren't seeing eye to eye about me.

"That's entirely beside the point, Chet."

"Well, what is the point?"

"My point is, if Opie is going to get serious about
something, it ought to be something concerning her
future. If she's going to teach some day, she should
be getting into some activity with children."

"When was it decided that Opie is going to teach?"
my Dad asked. "You have this fixed idea. Actually,
nothing has been settled at all."

"*I* have a fixed idea? It seems to me if anybody has
a fixed idea around here, it's you. Teaching at least is
something Opie can fall back on as a last resort if
times are hard and her husband isn't doing well ..."

My Dad groaned. "God knows our school systems are plagued with that kind of teacher," he said. "When I think that we give our kids over to people who are teaching as a last resort it makes me shudder."

"There are lots of fine dedicated teachers," my Mom said stiffly. She happens to think she's one of them.

"I agree. But I seriously doubt that either one of our girls would be in that category. Well, I take that back. I think Lissie will probably be a good phys. ed. teacher. But Opie . . ." my father's voice trailed off.

"She's wonderful with children," my Mom said firmly. "She was a wonderful counselor at camp last year." She was talking about the day camp the Center runs. "And look at the way she handles Marvin."

I just sat there listening, and I couldn't believe the way they were settling the future for me. I was going to get up and go in there, but then my Dad started talking again.

"I'm convinced Opie has the makings of a good social worker . . ."

"I can't see Opie as a social worker. It's so . . . grim!"

"If you were a Victorian mother, I'd expect you to faint. Come on, Elizabeth. It's a fine career. Maybe she should specialize in geriatrics. She's very good with old people."

I didn't know what to do. I had half a mind to go in there and stop them from getting into a fruitless quarrel. I mean, here I am, only in junior high school. I've got lots of time to make up my mind. Well, maybe not lots of time really, because by the time you're in high school, they start giving you all these career talks and people come to the school from different colleges, and it's push, push, push, all the time, to make some kind of a decision.

I decided to go back upstairs instead, and not even let on that I'd heard them. I sat down on my bed and stared at the window. Their whole conversation was being played over in my mind like a record.

I began to wonder. Had Lissie always wanted to be a teacher? Or had it just been my Mom, putting on the pressure. Oh, not coming right out and saying, "Lissie, you're going to be a teacher and that's that." My Mom isn't like that. But there are other ways to get your ideas across.

Did I want to be a teacher? I really tried to see myself someday, say in North Central, maybe an English teacher like Mrs. Humphreys. To be totally honest with you, the whole idea turned me off. My

Dad's right about that. It's my Mom's dream, not mine. On the other hand, did I want to be a social worker? In *geriatrics*? Nothing but old people around me? Did I want to work in a place like Maple Ridge? All of a sudden, all I could see was Mabel Yore's face — not Mrs. Sherman or Mrs. Lee or Mr. Smithers — just Mabel Yore. And I got scared. I really did.

I grabbed my panda (I don't care if it does seem silly, someone my age still holding on to an old stuffed toy), and I stretched out on the bed and just held on to that beat-up toy animal as tight as I could.

And I made up my mind. When I went back to Maple Ridge tomorrow, I was going to quit. I didn't want to be a volunteer anymore. I didn't want to be involved in *anything* anymore. I just wanted to be fourteen years old, that's all.

I squeezed the panda up against my face, the way I used to when I was real little, and for no reason I could think of, I just suddenly began to cry.

Chapter Seven

I still felt the same way the next morning. My mother thinks if you have a problem, you should "sleep on it," as if something magical will happen during the night and the problem will go away. I guess she agrees with my Dad that I'm too impulsive, only I didn't feel I was being impulsive now.

Anyway, I just said right out at breakfast that I was going to quit being a volunteer at the Home.

"It's about time," Lissie said. "I don't know how you stuck it out this long."

"Oh, shut up!" I yelled at her.

She got mad. "Don't take your guilt feelings out on me, Penelope Cross," she yelled back.

"I am not feeling guilty," I said, but of course I was. She didn't answer me, just gave me this knowing smile, and that made me even madder.

"All right, girls," my Dad said quietly.

I waited for him to comment on my decision but he didn't say a word.

My Mom opened her mouth but closed it again when my Dad gave her a forbidding look. I suppose he felt whatever she said would only rub me the wrong way. I knew she was glad and my Dad was disappointed because my mother's eyes were bright and shining, and my Dad got this distant, withdrawn expression he has when he disagrees with what you're doing but will defend to the death or something your right to make your own mistakes.

I got up from the table.

"Where are you going, Opie?" my Mom asked.

"Over to Maple Ridge. I've got to tell them . . ."

"Oh, Opie. That isn't necessary, dear. Just call Mrs. Orrmont on the phone . . ."

"NO!" my Dad exploded. "She will not call Mrs. Orrmont on the phone, Elizabeth. She will go to Maple Ridge, as she should, and make her explanations in person. She owes them that . . ."

"She's only a volunteer, Chet. It's not as if she's getting *paid,* for heaven's sake."

"Volunteers are not immune to obligations . . ."

"We're not in a courtroom, Daddy," Lissie said. She hates what she calls his attorney-at-law voice. "Besides, if Opie goes back there, they'll try to talk her into staying on. And you know what a pushover Opie is for a sad story."

I guess I secretly agreed with Lissie, I mean that they would try and talk me out of quitting. But Mrs. Orrmont didn't try at all, and neither did Mr. Ver Lees. He happened to be in her office when I went in.

"We certainly appreciate all you've done for us while you were here," Mr. Ver Lees said.

"You've been just wonderful, Opie," Mrs. Orrmont said warmly. "Our residents will miss you, of course. But they're used to having you girls come and go."

Did I tell you there were about five of us candy-stripers who started this summer at Maple Ridge? Two of the girls were only twelve — Mary Palmer and Janet Dancer. Mary only stayed two weeks, but Janet is still there. And Sandy Roux and Melinda Becker. Sandy's the one who brought a record player from home and set it up for Mrs. Lee. She put the records in this special order so Mrs. Lee would know what she was going to hear. I told you Mrs. Lee doesn't see very well, didn't I? And she brought her some talking books — she borrows them from the School for the Blind. What happens at the Home is that we all have certain favorites — I mean, we kind of like some people more than others, and we get more involved with them, the way I was involved with Mrs. Sherman.

We all still have to visit with the other residents,

of course, or it wouldn't be fair. And we have to take them back and forth to wherever they want to go, out on the porch, or down to the arts-and-crafts room — stuff like that. And I write letters for Mr. Davidson and Mr. Permaloft.

Melinda's the one who thought about having a beauty shop at Maple Ridge. It's not much, just a little room with two sinks and two dryers in it. Melinda's mother owns a beauty shop, so Melinda got this idea about wouldn't it make some of the women feel marvelous to have their hair washed and set. My Dad said that psychologically the benefits would be enormous. Melinda's mother comes in every Monday morning — that's the day her shop is closed — and she and Melinda work in that little room all day. Sandy and Janet and I bring in coffee. I sometimes think that's the happiest room in the building, even though it looks like a dingy closet.

We've had three new girls since Mary left. One of them quit the first day.

So that's what Mrs. Orrmont meant when she told me the residents didn't expect the candy-stripers to last long.

"Do you want to leave now?" Mr. Ver Lees asked me. "Or will you stay just for today and help us with the birthday party?"

The birthday party! I had forgotten all about it. Today was Mr. Handy's eighty-eighth birthday. You remember Mr. Handy? The gentle kleptomaniac who takes the silverware?

The women in the Maple Ridge Guild always have birthday parties for the residents. The people in the kitchen bake a special cake, and the Guild buys a birthday present and wraps it up in pretty paper with ribbons and all, and Mrs. Orrmont plays the piano (she is the *worst* pianist in the whole wide world; she jams her foot down on the pedal and every note comes out a horrendous fortissimo) and the residents sing along. You can hear all this noise clear out to the street.

Well, I naturally wasn't going to walk out on Mr. Handy's birthday party, so I said I would stay. Mrs. Orrmont called all of us candy-stripers together and told us which ones were to be in charge of handing out the cake, which ones were to pour the lemonade, who was to help with the decorations — they always hang up crepe paper and paper ornaments — and who was to take care of setting up the chairs in the living room. I helped with the decorations and then I was the one who had to make sure the residents came. They're very forgetful, some of them, and if they missed the party, they would be fretful all day.

The party wasn't going to take place until after lunch because if everybody got cake and lemonade before lunch, nobody would be able to eat. But this wasn't one of my afternoons at the pool, so I could stay and help.

It was fun. The residents get all excited at birthday parties, I guess because it gives them something different to do.

When the living room was all fixed up in the afternoon, Mrs. Orrmont and the other members of the Guild looked around to make sure everything was ready — enough seats and the paper birthday tablecloth on the serving table, and plenty of paper cups and plates — you know, the whole bit — and then she told me to go and get the residents who were still in their rooms.

They all came, smiling and anxious to get the cake and candy (Mr. Ver Lees is kind of strict about too many sweets, so they do get greedy at these parties), and some of them were all dressed up. The only one who refused to come was Mrs. Longwood.

"No, Opie, I will not attend," she said, holding up her head very proudly. "You just go ahead and enjoy yourself. Without me."

"Oh, Mrs. Longwood. You're the best singer here." I wasn't just buttering her up. She really does have a good, true voice. I think she's the only one who keeps the rest of them somewhere in vague reach of the melody. "Why won't you come?"

"Ask my guardian," she said.

I stared at her. Mrs. Longwood does quite a few odd things, and she sometimes says even odder things, but this time she sounded really peculiar. I mean, guardians are people who take care of little kids and orphans, right?

So I repeated it, just to make sure that was what she really said. "Guardian?"

"You don't know what I'm talking about. Well, I'll tell you, and you just sit there and listen and learn so when you get old you won't be as foolish as I am. When I came to Maple Ridge, my nephew Clarence talked me into making him my absolute guardian. Do you know what that means?"

I didn't answer, but it wouldn't have made any difference, because the words were tumbling out of her mouth like water rushing over a cliff.

"It means I gave Clarence the right to act for me, to make decisions for me, to tell me what I can or can't do with my money. Now when I want something, I have to ask Clarence Longwood ... *beg* my nephew ... Is there any reason I can't buy a new dress if I want to?" she demanded. "Or half a dozen new dresses? It's my money. Do you know what Clarence had the nerve to tell me. I don't need a dress for this party, he said. Now I ask you, Opie. What difference does that make? A woman doesn't have to *need* a dress to buy one. The man's a fool!"

She looked away from me and stared out the window.

"He persuaded me to appoint him my guardian when I first came here. Said he would safeguard my money. Make wise investments. At my age, who cares? I've been sensible all my life, had to be. Because it was always for the future, you see. Well, the future is here, and I wouldn't give you two cents for it."

"Can't you un-appoint him?" I asked.

She turned back to me and patted my hand.

"Go to court and maybe have my nephew tell everybody I'm senile and incompetent? Maybe have him win?"

She jumped up.

"I've got to walk."

She pushed me aside and started moving down the corridor. I ran after her.

"Mrs. Longwood. You can't . . ."

But she was off and running, with me chasing after her. She went out the back door so the others didn't see her. You wouldn't believe how hard it was for me to catch up with her, she moved so rapidly. Now I knew why Mrs. Longwood went tearing off up Central. It was the way she worked off her anger at her guardian.

"Wait, Mrs. Longwood. I'll walk with you," I yelled after her.

I grabbed her hand when I caught up with her. "Listen, Mrs. Longwood," I said. "My Dad's a lawyer. He'll be able to help you, give you some advice."

"What can your father do? Talking to Clarence would be a waste of time."

"He'll talk to you. He'll tell you what your rights are."

"Old people don't have any rights . . ."

"Not if they're stubborn and won't listen," I snapped.

She stopped walking. I thought she was going to get really angry. Instead, she started grinning.

"My, you're a real little peppercorn, aren't you, Opie? All right. You get your father to come and talk to me."

She squeezed my hand.

"No sense missing out on the cake and other goodies, Opie. Let's go back."

The noise of the party was still going strong. No one even noticed that we hadn't been there right along. I went and got some cake for Mrs. Longwood, and took a piece for myself, too. After I got Mrs. Longwood settled, I went and sat down on the stairway with my cake.

In a few minutes, Sandy Roux came and sat down beside me. She peered out at the residents through the banisters.

"They're so grateful, it's pathetic," Sandy said, after a while. She took a bite of her cake. "You going to help out at the Family Fair?" she asked. Then she added quickly, "Oh, I forgot. You're quitting, aren't you?"

The Family Fair. It was always the big money-making event of the year for Maple Ridge. I honestly couldn't leave before then, could I? Well, why not? Why couldn't I? Why couldn't I just walk away from it all if I wanted to?

I felt disagreeable and mad and guilty, so naturally I took it out on Sandy. "Why don't you just mind your own business for once?" I flared up at her.

She started to answer me, but then she changed her mind. She just got up and left.

I put my dish with the cake down on the step. I suddenly felt if I took another bite, it would choke me.

Chapter Eight

I wish Mrs. Humphreys was here, instead of off in Mexico or Europe or some island in the Atlantic or Pacific. That's what she does every summer — makes these pilgrimages to wherever some famous author lived. She's actually been in Hans Christian Andersen's house, and Byron's home in Italy, and who knows where all.

If Mrs. Humphreys was here, she would tell me what to tell you next — I mean, in the proper way. I want to tell you about the Fair, mostly.

I know I said I was quitting as a volunteer, but I found out I really couldn't, after all. I mean it just didn't seem like the right time to walk out on them.

When I mentioned this at supper, Mom sighed. "When will you stop letting your heart rule your head?" she asked me.

"Heart! Head!" my Dad practically snorted. "Opie simply has a sense of responsibility . . ."

"I am so sick of hearing about the Home," Lissie yelled. "Can't we ever talk about anything else?"

"Well I thank the good Lord this will all be over soon," my Mom said, "I can't wait for the summer to be over and school to open again." From the look she gave me, I knew she expected me to be studying my head off so I could make good grades so I could get into a good college and wind up being a teacher. My Mom doesn't give up very easily.

"All right," my Dad put in quietly, "I suggest we all simmer down." And then he steered the conversation in a different direction.

The Fair was important though, and I really do want to tell you about it. But I can't till I tell you about the turtle race, and I can't do *that* until I explain about Marvin. I suppose Mrs. Humphreys would tell me to lay the foundation again, so that's what I'll do.

Well, you remember that the Peppers lived on one side of us and the Goldsmiths on the other. I think the Goldsmiths are kind of ancient to have a little kid like Marvin — he's only seven — and Judge Goldsmith is three years older than my Dad, who is forty-four! They have three grown-up children — two married and one in college. So the way it's worked out, with Marvin being so little and the Goldsmiths being so old and all, is that Marvin is spoiled rotten. You wouldn't believe the mischief that that one little kid gets into. Like the time he and Pat Crystal — she's another little kid that lives across the street, in that house that's right at the dead end — locked themselves in the bathroom.

I was baby-sitting for both of them. When I tried to open the door, I could hear them giggling. I yelled, "What are you two doing in there? You open this door this minute, you hear?"

Do you know what they were doing?

They were playing basketball! I swear! Marvin and Pat were tossing oranges into the toilet bowl. Mrs. Goldsmith didn't think it was very funny, but when my Dad heard about it, he practically turned purple trying not to laugh. Then he and Judge Goldsmith grinned at one another, and the Judge said, "Who knows? Maybe Marvin will make it to the big leagues some day."

I personally fail to see Marvin's charm, but then I have to baby-sit every time the Goldsmiths go some-where. That's what happens when your parents are good friends as well as neighbors, and one family has this little kid and the other family has this daughter who is practically a slave to their whims.

This is the end of the foundation. So now I can get back to the Family Fair. I was visiting Mrs. Sherman the day after the birthday party and we were talking about the Fair. There's this big backyard behind Maple Ridge, and the Guild was planning to set up all kinds of booths. There was going to be a White Elephant Booth — that's for all the junk people don't want that they donate. White Elephant booths are popular because one person's junk is another person's absolute treasure. I remember the time, for instance, my Dad forced my Mom to donate a cut-glass vase to the rummage sale at the church, which he thought was a monstrosity — the vase, not the church, of course — and Mrs. Rice squealing when she caught sight of it and paying ten dollars for it! And when my Mom looked daggers at my Dad, because she thinks Mrs. Rice has such good taste, my Dad just shrugged and said, "So now it's a ten-dollar monstrosity."

One of the booths was going to have handmade items the residents were contributing. Mrs. Sherman made this beautiful afghan for the Boutique Booth. And there's the Fix-It Booth. Mr. Smithers thought of that. He says it's a damn shame how many things people throw away that can be repaired. And Mr.

Pepper thought up the Wheel of Fortune, so he was going to run that.

I mean, there really were some neat things to look at and buy and do.

Anyway, Mrs. Sherman and I were talking about the Family Fair and somehow she got to reminiscing about the olden days.

"We used to have block parties," she said, sort of dreaming. "They were such fun."

"What's a block party?" I asked, which was a perfectly reasonable question since I'd never heard of one before.

"Do you mean to say you've never been to a block party?"

Now why do people do that? Would I have asked if I had been to one?

She explained how they used to close off a block by placing barriers on each end of the street. Then they would have an all-day party, and sometimes late into the night. They would set up stands (they didn't call them booths in those days, she said), and all the women in the block would make different kinds of food. And there would be games, like two people racing with one foot each in the same potato sack, or pushing a peanut along the street with their noses.

Listening to Mrs. Sherman, I began to get all excited. Why couldn't we have the Family Fair as a block party? A lot of people don't want to come to Maple Ridge, even if it's to an outside event. But I bet they would come to a block party. And there would be so much more room.

After I left Mrs. Sherman, I ran into Mrs. Orrmont's office. I must have been talking a mile a minute because she said, "Slow down, Opie."

She listened — she had a rubber band that she was twirling on her two forefingers — and then she shook her head.

"Where would we hold it? And how would we get permission to close off a street? And it would mean trundling the residents over there, which would mean getting volunteers to drive them there and back . . ."

I kept after her, knocking down her objections one by one. While I was persuading her, Mr. Ver Lees came in and stood with his back against the door. He didn't say anything, just stood there.

I said I didn't know if they let you close off a street anymore, but my Dad would know. Sometimes it is very convenient to have a father who is a lawyer. There could be a lot more booths. We have lots of artists in Indianapolis, and they're always looking for new places to display their work. They could come and show their paintings and sculpture and whatever, and pay a fee to the Guild for showing their work.

Guild members could bring their baked goodies to the block party just as well as to the backyard at Maple Ridge. And maybe the women on the block would bake, too. And of course there would be games. People could come to the block party free. But whoever entered a game would have to pay a small fee.

"Lots of people would come to a block party who wouldn't come to Maple Ridge," I insisted. "We could advertise it in the *Topics* (that's a local paper we have that has all these ads for garage sales and things).

"Opie has a point, Birdie," Mr. Ver Lees said when I stopped to catch my breath.

Mrs. Orrmont had stopped fooling around with the rubber band and was drawing boxes. That meant she was taking me seriously.

"I suppose we *could* get the residents over there. We'd need a couple of cab-ulances for the ones in wheel chairs. That would be expensive . . ."

"I can get them to donate their services just for this one time," Mr. Ver Lees said positively.

"What block are we talking about?" Birdie Orrmont asked.

"My block," I blurted out. "It would be just perfect, seeing how it's a dead-end street and all."

"Will you talk to your father? We haven't much time to arrange it. And we'll have to get flyers out, announcing it."

"I'll talk to my Dad tonight. He'll arrange it. You'll see."

Mr. Ver Lees and Mrs. Orrmont gave each other amused glances.

"Sounds like you think your father can move mountains," Mr. Ver Lees teased.

"Many a truth is said in jest," Mrs. Orrmont told him.

Well, maybe it is. Because I happen to think my Dad is a man who can get things done if he has a mind to. And he did have a mind to, when I spoke to him that night. He said right away it would be no problem at all. As a matter of fact, he made a few phone calls, came back nodding his head, and told me I could give Maple Ridge the green light on the block party.

Even my Mom flipped. She got on the phone and started to call the neighbors. Before she made too many, I explained that she would have to clear her plans with Mrs. Orrmont, because after all, this was still for the benefit of the Home. She said she understood, and I thought she would go down to Maple Ridge and talk to Mrs. Orrmont. But I underestimated my Mom. She wouldn't set foot in Maple Ridge for all the tea in China, she insisted. So Mrs. Orrmont agreed to come to our house, along with the officers of the Guild, to plan the party.

The next night there they were, in our living room, plotting every move. My Dad was hiding in the den. I'd been in the living room to greet Mrs. Orrmont and the others and I started to leave the room. That was when Mrs. Orrmont looked up and said firmly, "Opie, why don't we put you down in charge of some games for the children?"

Now you look at that statement. Is that or is that not a question? You're right. It is not a question. Mrs. Orrmont's voice always goes up like that at the end of a sentence. She doesn't expect an answer.

"All right. We have Opie in charge of the children's games. Now I think we ought to put Maggie Jimson in charge of adult games ... she's *very* organized ..."

When I went out of the room, my Mom and the other ladies were all talking at the same time and busy scribbling notes on their pads. From the way their voices sounded, you'd think they were controlling the destiny of nations.

I went up to my room and was sitting in my chair brooding, trying to think of some games for kids that wouldn't tax their little brains but wouldn't be too totally boring. And in walked Marvin. He just walked into the room where I was sitting with my eyes closed so I could concentrate, put his lips right up close to my ear, and yelled, "OPIE!"

I thought I was going to die! My heart tried to jump right out of my body. When my breath came back I told him, "Marvin, if you ever sneak up on me again like that, I will turn you inside out and throw you to the wolves."

"We don't have wolves in Indiana," he told me. Practical Marvin. See what I mean about Mrs. Goldsmith? No wonder Marvin was so entranced with the leprechaun tree. No whimsy for Marvin, Mrs. Goldsmith told me very firmly. I want him to know it like it is. Reality. Truth.

"Then I'll take you to Florida," I snapped, "and feed you to the alligators."

He looked at me with those big brown eyes and said very seriously, "And then afterward, Opie, can we go to Disney World?"

"Marvin," I said. "What are you doing here anyway? You should be home and in bed."

"My Mommy's downstairs."

"You don't need your mother. You're a big boy, Marvin. You just run along and go home. I'm busy."

"No, you're not, Opie. You're not busy. You're just sitting in your chair."

"My body isn't busy. It's my brain that's busy."

So Marvin stared at my head, trying to see my brain at work. He even put one of his hands on my head and pushed my hair to one side, but he still couldn't see my brain. Seven-year-old kids!

"Marvin," I yelled. "Will you get out of here?"

"First I have to show you what I have," he insisted, and he opened his hand. "Isn't he beautiful?"

"Yuch!" I said. What Marvin had was a little old ugly turtle, gasping for breath from the inside of Marvin's palm. Naturally I told him to get that ugly creature out of my room, and out of my house, and naturally Marvin didn't budge. Instead, he put the turtle on the floor.

"Look at him go, Opie," Marvin said.

Listen, if I'd been that turtle, I'd have gone any-where to get away from Marvin, too. But watching that turtle crawl along the floor gave me this great idea. Why not have a turtle race for the little kids at the block party? A lot of kids have turtles. And those that don't have those yuchy little creatures can get them at a pet shop. We could charge the kids an en-

trance fee. I could just see the banner I would make
... First Annual Horizon Drive Turtle Race.

"Is your brain getting busy again, Opie?" Marvin
asked, staring at me. Too bad for Marvin that I wasn't
the visible woman so he could look inside my head
and see the wheels going around. I was going to tell
Marvin to go on home, and then I thought — he did
give me this idea. So instead of chasing him out, I
just said, "You want me to read a story to you,
Marvin?"

Marvin's eyes got all shiny. He loves to have me
read to him, especially since the books I have from
when I was little are so different from the kind of
books his mother thinks Marvin should have.

"You're my best friend in the whole world, Opie,"
Marvin said.

Which I am not! But why should I destroy a little
kid's illusions?

Chapter Nine

The block party day turned out to be just perfect, sunny but with enough feathery-soft white-spun clouds passing by overhead so that the sky looked like a picture postcard.

Lissie helped me paint lines in the space for the turtle race so each turtle would have its own runway. That was before everybody came, of course, because afterwards it would have been impossible there were such hordes of people who must have read about it in the *Topics*. And then there were all these little kids holding their turtles later on and coming up every few minutes to ask when the race was going to start.

The Guild women and the people on our block and some of the residents from Maple Ridge had spent the whole morning setting up the booths and stands. The calling back and forth and the chattering that went on and the hammering and what all made our little street look and feel like the site of the next World's Fair. All the candy-stripers were on hand, too, and I want to tell you we were really kept hop-ping.

I walked up and down the street before the Family Fair started and I was amazed. There was the usual White Elephant table with a lot of ratty old stuff, but the Boutique Booth had beautiful handmade sweaters, berets, and scarfs and stuffed crocheted dolls and animals I didn't think anybody could resist. Further on, there was the Green Thumb Booth, which was Mr. Georgeby's idea. He has this thing about plants — always repotting them and fertilizing and encouraging them. Mrs. Orrmont says all Mr. Georgeby has to do is put a seed in the ground and it comes up like a tree but when she puts a seed in the ground it lies there and sulks.

Even Lissie got into the spirit of the Fair. She got some of the kids from the school band to come over, and they were down at the end of the block, playing dance music. Lissie and some of the other cheer-leaders were livening things up, strutting around yell-ing, "Give me an M, give me an A, give me a P–L–E; give me an R, give me an I, give me a D–G–E."

It was noisy, but it was fun.

There were even some game booths scattered around. And there were places to eat. The women on our block had set up some porch and patio furniture as sidewalk cafes. They were serving hot dogs and hamburgers and cold drinks.

It looked like a movie set, it was so bright and busy. Cars filled with people from Maple Ridge kept coming and going.

Mrs. Longwood was over at the Boutique Booth with Mrs. Sherman. I was going past when Mrs. Longwood called me back. Her eyes were sparkling. I don't think I'd ever seen her so happy.

"Your father came to see me last week," she told me. I suppose I must have looked blank because she said impatiently, "Don't you remember my telling you about Clarence, my guardian?"

"Oh yes. Your absolute guardian!"

"Your father explained that I could get another guardian because my nephew, being my only living kin, will inherit everything when I die, so his being my guardian constitutes a conflict of interest," she said in a triumphant voice. "And he explained that a judge would probably find that I didn't understand the basis of what I was doing when I made Clarence my absolute guardian, which I didn't, because butter wouldn't have melted in Clarence's mouth the day he talked me into appointing him."

"That's great," I told her and started to move away because honestly there were so many things I had to do, but she kept right on talking. You know how some older people trap you in a net of words, talking very fast while you're trying to escape? You just can't walk away when someone's still speaking.

"Your father said the court would take into consideration that I misunderstood the powers I was conveying to my nephew. And furthermore, he wasn't fulfilling his duties if he didn't realize that my emotional needs were just as important as my physical needs, and that when he wouldn't let me buy a dress when I wanted to, or take some of my friends at Maple Ridge out to dinner because it was too expensive, he was subjecting me to emotional stress."

"I'm glad it's all settled, Mrs. Longwood," I told her, thinking I could get away now.

"It's not settled at all, Opie. I still have to go to court. But your father agreed to represent me. He gave me this whole list of lawyers he said I could choose from that he could vouch for, and I said, 'What's wrong with you, Chester Cross?' Your father took a lot of persuading, but I know an honest man when I see one. It's not that Clarence isn't honest, my dear. It's just that he hasn't got the sense he was born with!"

She turned around and said to Mrs. Sherman, "Not letting me have a dress for Mr. Handy's birthday.

That was the straw that broke the camel's back. After all, as Mr. Cross said, it wasn't as if I was living in the middle of a desert and demanding money for a boat!"

While she was talking to Mrs. Sherman, I sneaked off. I figured that wasn't exactly the way my Dad probably put it. Besides, if you want my frank opinion, I think Mrs. Longwood might very well suddenly want a rowboat in the middle of a desert on the grounds that you never knew when you might come across an oasis or something.

I don't want you to think I wasn't glad my Dad was going to help Mrs. Longwood because I really was. The only thing was, I had my mind on other matters just then, particularly the race.

Mr. Pepper was over at the Wheel of Fortune, acting like a barker at a carnival. You know — these guys that say "Hurry! Hurry! Hurry! See the little lady do the dance of death with a cobra! Hurry! Hurry! Hurry!"

When I came by, Mr. Pepper was shouting, "The Wheel of Fortune goes, and where she stops, nobody knows. Step up, ladies and gentlemen. Come closer, young friends. Keep your eye on the Wheel of Fortune!"

When he saw me, he grinned. "Isn't this a beautiful day, Opie?" He didn't wait for an answer. He just took a deep breath and went on, "I'm out in the real world again! Think of it. People of all ages milling about, free to come and go. I feel real again myself, and not like a nonperson." There was a bunch of people pushing up to the Wheel of Fortune, and Mr. Pepper got too busy to talk to me, for which I was thankful because time was getting on, and I had to get over to the raceway.

At two o'clock I blew my whistle and announced that all the kids who were entered in the race were to come over and get their numbers. I was just handing out the numbers as they came up. I mean a number is just a number, right? Wrong! Because Pat Crystal (the oranges in the toilet bowl kid) refused to take her number, which was eight. Eight wasn't a lucky number for a turtle race, she said, nice and loud and clear, and she wanted number thirteen which was a lucky number because she was born on the thirteenth.

Well, if you let them, kids like that will take over the world. So I just told her very firmly she would have to take her chances, the same as everybody else. She ran away crying and came back with her mother.

"I really don't see, Penelope," Mrs. Crystal's voice

was just dripping icicles, "why Pat can't have number thirteen, as long as she has her heart set on it."

I started to explain, but meanwhile the other kids were beginning to yell that they wanted to pick their own numbers, too. It felt like I was going to have a kid riot on my hands. I could see the First Annual Horizon Drive Turtle Race was also going to be the Last Annual Horizon Drive Turtle Race if I didn't get things in hand right away. So I blew my whistle again, hard. When the kids got quiet, I said (in the same voice my Dad uses when he says "Penelope!"), "If there is any more hassle about numbers, this race will be called off, RIGHT NOW!"

Listen, I do enough baby-sitting to know that kids have you at their mercy if you show them a minute's weakness.

Mrs. Crystal gave me a frosty look and went to stand at the end of the turtleway. "Never you mind, dear," she told Pat before she went off. "Mother feels number eight will be very lucky today."

Lissie and I had worked very hard trying to get things professional for the race. We made up the numbers in different colors, and we made up matching numbers for the kids to paste on the backs of their turtles. When all the numbers were handed out and pasted on, I blew my whistle again and told the contestants to line up with their turtles. Lissie had helped me chalk in the numbers at the head of each line, and all the kids had to do was to match themselves and their turtles against the numbers on the lanes.

Mrs. Sherman had turned over the Boutique Booth to Mabel Yore for a while (I bet business hit rock bottom), and she came over to help. She was very businesslike; she had brought an old notebook and she wrote down the name and address of each kid who had entered the race, and the name of the turtle. She was having a wonderful time.

I looked around to see if everyone was ready. A lot of parents and older brothers and sisters were lined up along the turtleways, and some of them were standing near the finish line. I was surprised to see Mr. Pepper there, talking very earnestly to Mr. Crystal. I couldn't imagine what they could have to talk about, though of course Mr. Pepper was always real friendly with Tad Crystal, who is an engineer like Mr. Pepper used to be. Anyhow, there they all were, their eyes on the starting line as if the Indianapolis 500 Speedway were about to begin.

The kids took their places, and a kind of hush came over the crowd as they waited for the starting whistle. I waited a minute, just for the drama of it all. Then I blew, a long, loud, piercing sound.

The kids gave their turtles a little push and then they started jumping up and down, screaming and laughing and yelling to their turtles to get a move on. And the people standing and watching were like kids themselves. They were calling out, "Come on, Jupiter!" and "You can do it, Charlie!" and "Let 'er rip, Twister!" and "Look at them go!" Which was one hundred percent imagination, because those turtles were just crawling along, not knowing what to make of all the confusion.

One turtle wasn't moving at all. He hadn't even left the starting line yet. It was Marvin's turtle, and he was just sitting there like he'd made up his mind this was as good a place as any other and what was in it for him? The other end was no different from this end.

"Is he dead?" I asked Marvin. "You want to pull him out of the race?"

"Don't worry about Clarence Darrow, Opie," he said, giving me one of his innocent looks. I should have suspected something right then and there. "Clarence Darrow has never lost a race yet."

"Marvin, Clarence Darrow has already lost a race because if you will take a look, you will see that most of the turtles are more than half way to the finish line."

"Don't worry, Opie. I'll just whisper a magic word in Clarence Darrow's ear."

"You do that," I told him, shaking my head. It would take some kind of magic to make that creature move. I looked down toward the finish line. Mr. Pepper was shaking hands with Mr. Crystal, and the two of them were walking away toward the Crystal house. That's nice, I thought vaguely, Mr. Crystal's taking Mr. Pepper to his house for coffee or something. Mrs. Crystal was glued to the spot, yelling, "Hurry, Parsley. Hurry." The names people give pets!

I looked back to where Marvin was standing, right at the starting line. He had picked up his turtle and was whispering to him and kind of stroking him. Then he put him down, and that turtle took off like he'd been shot out of a cannon. I mean he was hurtling himself down that line like a gold medal was waiting for him at the other end. The way he passed the other turtles, you'd have thought they were standing still. A couple of them got so frightened when Clarence Darrow whizzed past that they bumped into each other and turned around and started coming back!

The next thing I knew, Clarence Darrow just

zoomed past the finish line, just ahead of Pat Crystal's turtle. Well, you know how kids are . . . sore losers. Pat started to cry.

"Mean, nasty old turtle," she yelled in a tantrum and knocked Clarence Darrow over with her foot. And then she stopped crying, like someone shutting a faucet off suddenly, and she gasped. A lot of the people standing there gasped, too . . . I guess you might call it a sort of a community gasp.

"The race was fixed!" some boy shouted as I came running over to the finish line. And wouldn't you know it was Gary Trivett, the guy I punched in the nose when we were in third grade. And it only proves that some things never change because I still felt like punching him in the nose, standing there and saying the race was fixed.

I looked down at Clarence Darrow and was absolutely and totally stunned. Marvin had put a small battery-operated car under his turtle. The race had been fixed, and under my very own eyes. Naturally there was only one thing to do, aside from rending Marvin limb from limb. I disqualified him on the spot and declared Pat's turtle, Parsley, the winner.

I must say that Judge Goldsmith was mighty wrathful. He asked Mrs. Sherman for her book with the list of names and addresses of all the turtle contestants, and later he made Marvin apologize, in person, while the Judge stood forbiddingly by, to each and every one of those kids and their parents, including Pat Crystal and her Mom and Dad.

Lissie said afterward, trying to make me feel better I suppose, "There's no use brooding, Opie. It was a perfectly good race and everybody had fun. And Marvin gave them something that they'll talk about for a long time. People love juicy things like this to happen."

As it turned out, Lissie was right about one thing — people do love juicy things to talk about, only it wasn't about the race. It was about what my Mom insisted upon calling the Rocking Chair Rebellion.

And none of it would have happened, some of the neighbors insisted, if it hadn't been for my wanting to have the block party.

Chapter Ten

The Rocking Chair Rebellion! The way my Mom used that phrase, you could almost see deep and dark plotting, with sinister figures meeting in out-of-the-way places, wearing trench coats and giving passwords out of the corners of their mouths like in the old-time movies.

Let me tell you what really started the Rebellion. It wasn't the block party, or the "FOR SALE" sign on the Crystal lawn. That was just the catalyst my Dad said, which is a fancy way of saying that the block party and the sign only served to speed up the action, that's all.

It began long before the block party, when Mrs. Sherman saw this article in the *Indianapolis News*. You wouldn't think such a small item, buried way in the back of the paper someplace, would even be noticed, much less saved. It was just a few lines about how some elderly people had rented a big old house and had turned it into a commune for senior citizens. That was in Chicago. Or maybe Los Angeles. Or St. Louis. I can't remember. Anyway, the whole point is, Mrs. Sherman began to talk about it.

"How I admire them, Opie," Mrs. Sherman said, giving me the clipping to read. "Think of these ten people just taking their courage in their hands and starting out fresh."

"Look. They call it a commune," I said, kind of surprised. "I thought only young people . . ."

She interrupted me. "I think you'll find, Opie, that the dictionary defines a commune as any group of people with similar interests and purposes who share property jointly."

"You mean they live together." I knew about that. I remember when Karen Japerson's sister Catherine ran off and her parents didn't know where she was for the longest time. Later they found out she was living in this commune in California. Karen said all the people in the commune were living together. They weren't married or anything. All they did was a lot of organic gardening and they hardly ever washed their hair. The Japersons went out to California and brought Catherine home. Only this fellow she was living with followed her, and now she and this guy are living together right in the Japerson house, which is on the corner of our street. You can just imagine how the neighbors talk about that. Mrs. Japerson just puts up this brave front. Whenever she talks about Catherine, she calls this fellow her "son-out-law," because she says she can't very well call him her son-in-law. She always smiles when she says it, but you can see she is really hurting.

I told Mrs. Sherman about Catherine Japerson, which made her feel pretty sober.

"I can assure you, Opie, that our commune would be somewhat different." I noticed how quickly she slipped into calling it "our commune."

"What commune is that?" said a voice from the doorway. Mr. Pepper was standing there, looking puzzled.

"Read this article, Simon, and tell me what you think about it."

He skimmed over it quickly.

"It would be lovely, Simon, wouldn't it? To have a place of one's own again? But of course it's impractical."

Mr. Pepper didn't think it was impractical. He took the whole idea seriously.

"What we would need would be three or four others to come in on something like this with us," he told her, kind of thinking out loud. "Someone like Smithers.

You know how he's always puttering around here, fixing things. And easy to get along with. That's very important. And Georgeby. That man would sell his soul to have his own garden again. Why, we could have home-grown vegetables all summer long."

That was true. Mr. Georgeby had started a vegetable garden out in the backyard at Maple Ridge. He brought tomatoes into the kitchen that were so big, they looked like red cantaloupes. And corn! Fresh from the stalks right into the pots.

I thought Mr. Pepper's idea of including Mr. Georgeby was terrific.

"If there were enough of us, we could pool our income," Mrs. Sherman said thoughtfully. "But what about the down payment on a house?" She sighed. "It's not as easy as this clipping makes you believe."

"Mrs. Longwood," I blurted out. "She's got pots of money."

"I don't think she can touch it. Not for something like this." Mrs. Sherman sounded doubtful.

"My Dad's her lawyer now," I said, all excited. "I bet he'd approve. He knows how unhappy she is at Maple Ridge."

"I'm not exactly a pauper myself," Mr. Pepper said. "We wouldn't need all that much from Madeline."

"I'll go get Mrs. Longwood," I offered and ran out

of Mrs. Sherman's room before either one could say anything. I really wanted them to try this commune thing. It wasn't the kind of idea that would work for most of the people at Maple Ridge, not the really old people, or the sick ones. Not for Mabel Yore, or even sweet old Mr. Handy, or Mrs. Lee. But for Mrs. Sherman and some of the others, the ones who were in pretty good shape physically and with minds still bright as new coins...

"What's the child talking about?" Mrs. Longwood demanded when I brought her to Mrs. Sherman's room. "What's this dreadful nonsense about living in some kind of communist community?"

"Commune, Madeline," Mr. Pepper corrected her. "Here. Don't say another word until you've read this article."

Mrs. Longwood read it once, then she read it again. Then she turned the article over and looked at the back of it, as if it could give her some additional information. "You mean to tell me that people our age have actually done this? They are actually living in this house, together? They are living the way they want to live?"

"The way Simon and I would like to live."

"But it takes a group," I said. I was so eager about it you'd have thought it was my idea in the first place.

"Who were you thinking of?" Mrs. Longwood asked, ignoring me.

"Georgeby, to take care of the grounds. Smithers, to do the handiwork around the house. And me. I'm a mighty handy man with tools myself. Serena to do some of the cooking."

I couldn't wait for Mr. Pepper to finish. "And you to help out with money for the down payment."

"I could take care of some of the housekeeping. Wouldn't it be grand to have a house to fuss over again?" Mrs. Longwood's face was all lit up. "Something to do with myself instead of playing cards and doodling around in the crafts room?"

"What would Mr. Ver Lees say?" Mrs. Sherman asked suddenly. "If we moved out, he might take it as a reflection on himself and how he runs Maple Ridge."

They all fell silent. They liked Mr. Ver Lees.

"Well," Mr. Pepper said after a while. "It was nice dreaming about it anyway."

I got so upset. It seems like people give up so easily. I guess I'm like my Dad; when I want something I kind of dig in my heels and fight for it. I shouldn't be so quick to judge, though. When you're old, it must get harder and harder to go against the establishment.

We sat around like mourners home from a funeral. Then it came to me that there was one very logical thing to do.

"Why don't you just go into Mr. Ver Lees' office and ask him? The worst thing that can happen is that he'll say he doesn't think much of the idea."

"He's the director of Maple Ridge. What other position can he take, for heaven's sake?" Mrs. Longwood said irritably.

"Opie's right," Mr. Pepper said. "It's about time we stood up to be counted." He turned to Mrs. Sherman. "There's no time like the present. Come along, Serena."

I tagged along like a fellow conspirator. I don't think they even noticed that I was there, they were so busy gathering up their courage to talk to Mr. Ver Lees.

Mr. Ver Lees was just on his way out, and he said he was terribly rushed and couldn't spare a minute, but when Mr. Pepper insisted, he sighed and they all went into his office. Me, too. He read the article. And he listened to them speak, interrupting each other because they were so anxious to get him to understand how important this was to them.

When they stopped talking, there was this long silence.

"You're against the whole idea, aren't you?" Mrs. Longwood snapped. "I might have known."

"Now Madeline," Mr. Ver Lees said mildly. "As a matter of fact, I've known about these communes for some time now. We do keep up with what's happening in our field, you know," he said with a smile. "I think it's the wave of the future. Not for everybody. We'll always have some people living in institutions of one kind or another. But we recognize the very real need for this particular type of housing for some of our active senior citizens."

"Then you wouldn't be against our trying to find a place of our own?" Mrs. Sherman asked quietly.

"You would have my wholehearted support. Some of you are here because you have had no other alternative. Now that you have found an alternative, I'll do whatever I can to help you."

I don't think I ever admired anybody more than I did Mr. Ver Lees just then. Except for maybe my Dad.

I wasn't around when they got their group together — Mr. Smithers, Mr. Georgeby, Mrs. Longwood, and Mrs. Gibson, who's one of the practical nurses at Maple Ridge. I know Mr. Pepper talked to a lot of real-estate agents about finding a house in the right area.

But how was I to know that Mr. Crystal would be putting his house up for sale, and that Mr. Pepper would spot it the day of the block party, and he and Mr. Crystal would get together and make a deal? I mean, I'm not a fortuneteller or anything.

Chapter Eleven

Do you realize that all of human history practically depends on one little word — *if?* If early men hadn't been hunters, they wouldn't have gone chasing mammoths or whatever across the Bering Strait. And if those early people hadn't wandered down across the continent of North America, we wouldn't have had any Indians. And if Columbus hadn't had this notion about the world being round, he wouldn't have come to America, and you know all the ifs you can figure out just from *that.*

Well, I want to tell you right now, when I look back over my whole life, that's the way it seems to me. I mean, just think about it a minute.

If I hadn't wrecked my Dad's car, I wouldn't have been up in my room, falling asleep out of sheer one hundred percent *ennui,* which is French for yawning yourself to death you're so bored. And if I hadn't waked up when I did, I wouldn't have seen Mr. Pepper sneaking out of his house in the dead of night. And I wouldn't have gone to Maple Ridge and met Mrs. Sherman or anything.

What got me started on all this iffy business was that three of the neighbors — John Hartman who lives next door to the Crystal house, and Mrs. Boight and Mrs. Anderson who live right across the street from the Crystal house — were sitting in our living room and fixing me with hard stares.

"If Opie hadn't persuaded us that the block party should be held on our street, none of this would have happened," Mrs. Boight said.

"It was Mrs. Sherman who found the clipping in the newspaper about this kind of commune," my Dad reminded Mrs. Boight. "And it was Mrs. Sherman who got the others interested in the idea. Opie and the block party had nothing to do with it."

"Well, I happen to believe Ida May is absolutely right," John Hartman boomed. "If we hadn't had the block party, Simon Pepper wouldn't have seen the 'for sale' sign on Tad Crystal's lawn, and we would never have been faced with this problem."

See what I mean about ifs?

"That's ridiculous on the face of it, John. Given the state of mind of some of the people at Maple

Ridge, and the natural yearning to have a place you can call your own, something like this was bound to happen." My Dad sounded very reasonable.

"We don't object to its happening," Mrs. Anderson said primly. "We just don't want that sort of thing on this street."

My Dad shrugged his shoulders. "It's kind of late in the day to stop it, isn't it? From what Tad Crystal told me, the deal has gone through."

"They certainly rushed it." Mrs. Anderson sounded bitter. "I must say I'm very surprised at Tad Crystal, selling his house that way, without any regard for how the people who will still be living here feel."

"He had to get it settled in a hurry," my Mom put in impatiently. "You know that he didn't want to go off and leave an empty house . . ."

"Better empty than . . ." Mrs. Boight gave a shudder that shook her whole body. You'd think the house had been turned over to Count Dracula.

"We're talking about those people coming in here and setting up a *commune*," Mr. Hartman boomed. "A *commune*, for God's sake!"

"There's nothing so powerful as an idea whose time has come, Mr. Hartman," I put in helpfully. I thought he would explode. All I was doing was quoting one of Mrs. Humphreys' favorite expressions.

I must have stared at that sentence thousands of times. Mrs. Humphreys has it tacked up on the wall behind her desk. It just suddenly seemed to me to fit, somehow.

"I think we can excuse Opie," Mr. Hartman said, glaring at me, waiting for me to leave the room.

Can you imagine? Wanting to throw me out of our own living room?

"She does live here," my Mom said frostily. She didn't like the way John Hartman spoke to me. She can talk to me any way she wants to, and she does, you better believe me. But let somebody else try it, and zing! she's a tiger defending her young.

Mrs. Anderson tried to smooth matters over. "You know we had a meeting of all the neighbors, Chet."

"We're sorry you couldn't be there. You would have found it very enlightening to know how everyone on the street feels about this," Mrs. Boight added.

"It was my sister's birthday," my Dad said.

"You could have called the meeting for another evening," my Mom said, sounding resentful. "You knew we were going out to dinner with Chet's family. I told you about it weeks ago."

Mrs. Anderson's voice got very tight. "We took a vote and decided to go to court to appeal the ruling of the Zoning Board."

My Dad didn't look pleased. He was the one who had told Simon Pepper and the others that they would have to get what he called a "variance" on the zoning regulations in our area.

Mrs. Boight and her group went before the Board and argued that the old people wanted to set up a rooming house.

They lost, but they weren't giving up, because here they were, asking my Dad and Mom to support their case in court.

Mrs. Boight said, in her tactful way, "After all, Elizabeth, we don't want those people coming in here and setting up a rooming house right on our street."

My Mom got mad, which surprised me because I always thought she didn't like the residents of Maple Ridge. But as she explained to me later, that wasn't it at all. She just hates the Home, hates any home for the aged. I guess the same is true for Mrs. Boight and Mr. Hartman and the other neighbors. It seems they have this deep-rooted fear . . . well, I can tell you about that some other time. Anyway, she snapped, "What do you mean by 'those people,' Ida May? You've known Simon Pepper for years."

Mrs. Anderson glared at my mother. "Are you going to sit there, Elizabeth, and tell us that a *com-*

mune right on our block wouldn't disturb you?" Mrs. Anderson stood up, she became so agitated. "Do you realize that not one of them is married? To each other, I mean?"

"Mr. Pepper and Mrs. Sherman would like to get married," I said, trying to be helpful again, "but they're afraid of what will happen to their Social Security payments."

"Young lady, do you understand what you're saying?" Mr. Hartman asked coldly.

"She's saying that these six people stand to lose part of their Social Security payments if they get married. Always assuming, of course, as you seem to be doing, that they plan on *living* together. Other than just sharing the same premises."

My Dad thought I didn't know what he meant by "living together," which in today's world is hard to believe. I mean, I could tell you stories about some of the girls in school that would curl your hair, as my Mom says. But that Mr. Hartman and Mrs. Anderson and Mrs. Boight would even think something like that about the residents made my blood boil. I thought Mr. Hartman and the other two were disgusting.

"Do we take this to mean that you are not on our

side in this matter?" Ida May Boight inquired, her lips pulled together in such a tight line it was a wonder her voice could get through.

"I hadn't planned on taking sides," my Dad began.

My Mom interrupted. "You can take it to mean that if Simon Pepper wants that house, Chester and I will do whatever we can to help him."

My Mom looked beautiful to me then, she honestly did, all fire and flame, defending Simon Pepper's rights.

"Never mind, Ida May," John Hartman reassured her. "It's purely academic anyway. I'm positive the court will overrule the Zoning Board's decision."

"You're not going to go through with this, are you, John?" My Mom couldn't believe that he was so worked up about the whole thing.

"Am I ever," he said frostily. "I will take them to court and I will fight them tooth and nail. I will not have that sort of place next door to me. I promise you that!"

"If that's the mean way you're going to act," I shouted, "then okay, we'll see you in court."

"Do be quiet," Ida May Boight told me sharply.

Dad walked over to me and put his arm around my shoulders.

"I think Opie has said it for us," he told her, giving my shoulder a little squeeze. "If that's the way you want it, well then, yes. We'll see you in court."

I thought Mrs. Sherman and the others would be glad to know that my Dad was going to fight for their rights, and they were. But they were also a little scared, too.

"Maybe we should look around for a house someplace else," Mr. Georgeby said. He's such a peaceable man. It must come from being at one with nature all the time.

"No," Mr. Pepper said stubbornly. "I know the neighborhood. I like that street. And I like the house. It's just right for us."

"And we have the best lawyer in town," Mrs. Longwood said. "I hope you're proud of your father, Opie."

"Oh, I am," I told her. I wasn't just saying that, either. I was proud of my Dad. And my Mom, too.

But it was more than that. I remembered how awful I felt the day my Mom and Dad were arguing about my future, my Mom wanting me to be a teacher, and my Dad wanting me to be a social worker. All of a sudden it hit me. Why couldn't I be a lawyer, like my Dad? A lawyer for people who needed you when they were old and uncertain and pushed aside?

It was just a quick passing thought, and I wasn't all that sure about it. It would take a lot of soul-searching — that's Lissie's favorite expression these days — to find out if the law was really my thing. But right now, it gave me a good feeling.

Chapter Twelve

I swear I don't know how anything ever gets done in this country. Do you have any idea how long it takes for your case to come up in court? First there's all this legal stuff that goes on and on, the notices and the summonses and what all.

My Dad said we were lucky we only had to wait a month. Some of these things can drag out for as much as a year! A year! How could Mr. Pepper, Mrs. Sherman, and the others wait a whole year?

I was afraid I'd be back in school and miss the whole thing, but as it happened the case of *Hartman* vs. *Pepper* was scheduled for the last week in August.

I had never been in the City-County Building. I never had any reason to go there before. It's very handsome, even though parking is murder. We went up to the fifth floor — that's where the Circuit Courts are. By "we" I mean a whole bunch of us. Naturally some of the residents wanted to be there. It was almost like a picnic or some other outing. They were so exicted about going downtown. Mr. Ver Lees showed up, which surprised me; I don't know how he found the time. And Mrs. Orrmont. And some of the candystripers.

We practically filled all the seats in the courtroom, which isn't hard. The courtroom isn't all that big. We sat in these neat really comfortable chairs that are behind a railing that separates you from the real action. Straight ahead, on a raised platform, is the judge's desk, which is called a bench.

Over on the right, on another raised platform that was lower than the judge's bench, were twelve brilliant orange seats. They're for the jury, only *Hartman* vs. *Pepper* wasn't a jury case. It was going to be heard by Judge Ephraim Hydecker. On the other side of the room, opposite the jury box, were two tables and several chairs. My Dad was sitting at one of the tables, and Mr. Hartman's lawyer was sitting on the edge of the table, swinging his legs, laughing and joking with my Dad.

"I don't see why they're so friendly," Sandy Roux whispered to me. "They are on opposite sides."

"It's kind of like a club, Sandy," I whispered back. "They all know each other. But when they get up to talk to the judge, they'll sound like enemies. You wait and see."

130

I know that because that's exactly how lawyers act on television programs, calling the judge "Your Honor" in court and then if he tells them to see him in his chambers, they call him Bill or Joe or whatever.

After about twenty minutes the judge came out through a little door in back of the court. The clerk yelled "All rise," which took a little longer than usual, I imagine, because some of the residents can't get up or sit down again very quickly.

I was kind of disappointed. I expected to see the judge in a black flowing robe. He was wearing an ordinary business suit with a tie that looked home-made. He wore these funny-looking half glasses, the kind you look down through to read with, and over the tops of to see with. He was a short man with straight brown hair swept across his head in the style that tells you right off he's probably trying to hide a big bald spot. He had a no-nonsense, let's-get-on-with-it look on his face that worried me. He sure didn't look sympathetic. His voice matched his face — a little raspy and a lot impatient, as if there was a long day ahead of him and it was already dragging 'way behind time.

He ruffled some papers on his desk and then he looked over his glasses and asked, "Is counsel for the plaintiff here?" Schuyler Withers nodded. "Is counsel for the defendant here?" My Dad nodded.

I don't know why judges do that. All he had to do was look over at the tables and see them. I suppose they have to follow the standard procedures, even though it looks silly from where you're sitting in the back of the courtroom.

After both lawyers agreed they were present, Judge Hydecker made a little speech to the spectators, explaining that this was not a jury hearing but a trial by court (which was himself), that he would listen carefully to all the facts in the matter and from those facts make a judgment. That judgment, he added, generally took several days, or longer (some of the residents groaned when they heard that, but some of them were delighted since it would mean another trip downtown); on the other hand, he went on, he did on occasion hand down an immediate decision.

Schuyler Withers got up to address the court.

"He looks like he's been stretched on the rack," Sandy giggled. Mr. Withers was the tallest, skinniest man I'd ever seen, all arms and legs. Even his head was long and thin. You'd think a man like that would be homely, but he had enormous twinkly nut-brown eyes and the most cheerful face that warmed you inside.

"Your Honor," his opening statement began, "my client objects to the establishment of a rooming house adjacent to his property on a street zoned for one-family residences. We expect to prove that the house, presently known as the Crystal residence at four-fifty Horizon Drive, is not only to function as a boarding house, but as a commune for single people living together for immoral purposes."

Mrs. Longwood gasped. "Twaddle!" she called out. "Absolute twaddle!"

Judge Hydecker peered at her over his glasses and said sternly, "I will decide that, madam. Be quiet."

When it was my Dad's turn, he got up and said, "Your Honor, far from being a rooming house, as learned counsel contends, the Crystal residence is and will remain a one-family residence, as we expect to prove conclusively. As for the second charge, considering the age of those who will be sharing Mr. Pepper's residence, I think the term 'twaddle' describes the accusation exactly."

He turned away so Judge Hydecker couldn't see him and gave Mrs. Longwood a small smile.

The first witness called was John Hartman. I have to admit that Mr. Hartman looks and sounds impressive, like a banker, or the president of a company, or something. After a few ordinary questions by Mr. Withers, like who John Hartman was and where did he live and was his house next door to the residence hitherto known as the Crystal house, John Hartman was asked, "You claim that Mr. Pepper plans to turn the Crystal house into a commune?"

"I certainly do. People their age acting like that. What kind of an example are they to young people? What will happen to property values if we let Mr. Pepper come in and turn a perfectly good house into another Home for the Aged?"

"Objection, Your Honor," my Dad said. "Is Mr. Hartman going to call it one thing or another? He can't have it both ways."

"I don't care what it's called," Mr. Hartman snapped back before anybody could stop him. "I say a house like that is for younger people, people with a family, a *growing* family. What's wrong with Maple Ridge anyway? It's a fine home for old folks."

Schuyler Withers leaped into the breach.

"Mr. Hartman, are you alone in wanting your street maintained as a strictly residential area of one-family homes?" When Mr. Hartman told him that more than half the people on the block resented the idea of Mr. Pepper taking over the house, Mr. Withers went on, "And you did take the matter up with the proper authorities, in this case, the Zoning Board?" Mr. Hartman said yes, but the Board had granted a variance. "An absolutely irresponsible attitude," Mr. Hartman said, glaring at Mr. Withers as if it was his idea. "They wouldn't have made a decision like that for the streets they live on, you can bet your bottom dollar on that."

My Dad was getting ready to object but Mr. Withers hurried in with a question. "What happened then, Mr. Hartman?"

"We called a meeting of all the neighbors on the block . . ."

"With the exception of Mr. and Mrs. Cross?"

". . . with the exception of Mr. and Mrs. Cross because they had a dinner invitation they couldn't break."

"Yes. Go on, Mr. Hartman."

"We told everyone there that we were going to appeal the Zoning Board's decision, and we all agreed, since this is a democracy and the majority is supposed to rule," he said, with a fierce look at my Dad, "that we would take the matter to court and abide by the decision of the judge."

"All the neighbors at that meeting were in agreement?"

"Not at first, no. But as I said, they finally said they would accept a court ruling."

"Did you inform Mr. and Mrs. Cross of the outcome of the meeting?"

"We did. Mrs. Boight and Mrs. Anderson — they live on the block, too — were there with me. And Chester Cross decided to turn this into some kind of crusade."

Judge Hydecker frowned. "Just answer the question, Mr. Hartman, without indulging in personal asides. There's no jury to impress here, just me. And I don't impress easily."

"You feel the matter would have been dropped quietly if Mr. Cross hadn't intervened?"

"Yes, I do. I certainly do."

Later, Mr. Withers called Ida May Boight to the stand. This time he concentrated on the zoning. Would Mrs. Boight, for example, object if Mr. Pepper bought the house and lived in it alone, or if he were to marry, with his wife? Of course not. She liked Simon Pepper. Always had. Then there was nothing personal in her fight to keep Simon Pepper from purchasing the Crystal residence? Of course not. She just felt that it would wind up being a rooming house, that was the problem. She had nothing personal about rooming houses, either. They were perfectly fine, where they belonged. Where they did not belong was on Horizon Drive.

"Mrs. Boight," my Dad said, walking up to her and giving her a friendly smile, "do you know the Japersons?"

"They have the corner house. Corner of Horizon Drive and Steeple Court."

"Is that a one-family residence?"

"You know perfectly well that it is, Chester."

"Do the Japersons have a boarder?"

Mrs. Boight looked startled. "No," she said, sounding very interested. "Do they?" She caught herself. "Is this some kind of trap?"

"Do the Japersons have a daughter Catherine?" Yes, they did. And a daughter named Karen, too. My Dad thanked her for the information. "Is there a young man living in the Japerson household at the present time?"

Mrs. Boight's lips got tight. "That's sordid," she exclaimed, her face getting pink.

"There is a young man living in the Japerson household who is not a relative, who is not married to Catherine?"

"I certainly am not going to answer that," she said, turning her face away.

"It requires a simple yes or no," the judge said testily. "The witness will force herself to utter one syllable or the other."

She threw the judge a furious look. "Yes."

"Then we may safely call the young man a boarder? And if we have a boarder in a house on Horizon Lane, it may be assumed that at least one residence on the street might be termed a boarding house?"

"Your Honor. This line of reasoning is so far-fetched as to be ridiculous," Mr. Withers called out from his chair.

I didn't think it was ridiculous. I thought my Dad was marvelous even to come up with an idea like that. So did the people from the Home. They began to applaud him. Then they realized where they were and stopped before the judge had a chance to pound his gavel.

"I'm through with this witness," my Dad said.

"You can't make a summer out of one swallow, but I give you A for trying," Mr. Withers said in a voice that was supposed to be a whisper but reached everybody in the room.

I'm not going to go through the whole hearing because it just went on and on. First there were all the witnesses that Mr. Withers called, and then there were the witnesses that my Dad called, like Mr. Ver

Lees, who of course said he was in favor of what Mr. Pepper wanted to do.

When Mr. Withers cross-examined Mr. Ver Lees, he said, "As an expert, what do you think the chances are for this group of elderly," he put a lot of emphasis on elderly, "people making a go of this venture?"

Mr. Ver Lees shrugged. "Who's to say? It might work out very well. It might fail."

Mr. Withers pounced. "It might fail . . ."

"Your Honor," my Dad protested. "That's hardly the issue here . . ."

But Mr. Ver Lees was still talking. "However, that's not the point. The point is that they should have the same right to try something and succeed, or fail, just like anyone else."

Mr. Withers thought he would do better with Clarence Longwood because he agreed that his aunt had what he called her "eccentricities," and that he didn't see eye to eye with her on a number of things. When he said that, Mrs. Longwood began to mutter so loud Judge Hydecker gave her a stern look over his glasses. But Clarence Longwood went on to say that if his aunt preferred to live in this house with a group of her friends, why more power to her; she was strong and hale and maybe the change of atmosphere was exactly what she needed.

"And if this project fails, as Mr. Ver Lees indicated it might?"

"Is failure a dirty word?" Mr. Longwood demanded. He sounded very irritable. "It seems to me everyone's life is made up of a series of successes and failures. But all of this is pure conjecture. We won't know how it will work out until they've been given a chance to try, will we?"

"Nothing like family to stand by you when the chips are down," Mrs. Longwood said in a good, carrying voice.

Judge Hydecker looked at her again but he didn't say a word.

When Mrs. Sherman took the stand, she announced right away that she and Mr. Pepper were going to be married. She nodded at Mr. Pepper, her eyes soft and glowing, and he smiled back at her. I sat back in my chair and felt so good inside about the two of them.

When it was Mr. Pepper's turn on the stand, my Dad asked him, "Mr. Pepper, won't your house, in effect, be a boarding house?"

Mr. Pepper shook his head. With an absolutely straight face, he said, "Boarders? Certainly not. The home would belong to me and to my future wife,

Mrs. Sherman. As for Mrs. Longwood, Mr. Georgeby, Mr. Smithers, and Mrs. Gibson — why, we would be taking them on as helpers. Mrs. Gibson is a fine nurse and cook. She is willing to help us. And Mr. Smithers will too. He is an excellent handyman. And Mr. Georgeby already has made plans for the garden."

Nothing could shake Mr. Pepper, not even the sharp questions Mr. Withers got up to ask him.

Then both lawyers made their closing statements, which I don't remember word for word, because my mind was wandering. What I was thinking was lawyers start off by telling you what they're going to say, then they say it, and then they wind up the whole thing by telling you what they just told you.

Judge Hydecker was scribbling away all the time. I don't know what he was writing, but I got this feeling that he was doing what Mrs. Orrmont always does — drawing boxes and filling them in.

After a while, he looked up and said, "It is the opinion of this court that the Crystal residence, if purchased by the defendant Simon Pepper, would not become either a boarding house or a home for the aged. This court commends the spirit of these six *individuals*," he emphasized the word, "who in the best American tradition are attempting to build lives for themselves by dint of their own efforts and labor. The court finds in favor of the defendant Simon Pepper."

The judge got up and left the courtroom quickly. I guess he didn't want to have to stop us all from cheering.

Chapter Thirteen

I've been back in school a couple of months. I'm at
North Central now. There's something about being
in high school that makes you feel really different,
more grown up. After all, in a few more years, I'll
be a *senior*.

My Dad tells me I've changed. I've matured, he
says. I looked at myself in the mirror after he told
me that, and I didn't look any different on the outside. There was just the same old face staring back
at me. But you can't see what's going on inside you
by looking at a mirror.

When I think back over the past summer, I can
almost put my finger on when I began growing up.
It was the night Mr. Pepper was going to run away.

By the way, Mr. Pepper and Mrs. Sherman did get
married. I thought you'd like to know. My Mom
insisted on their having the ceremony in our house.
She invited some of the residents from Maple Ridge,
and some of the neighbors. I must say the neighbors

took the whole thing very well. My Dad feels a lot of them were ashamed of the way they fought having the Maple Ridge people come and live on our street. Not the three die-hards, of course. Mrs. Boight still looks the other way. And Mrs. Anderson and Mr. Hartman have "FOR SALE" signs up on their lawns.

But a lot of the other neighbors have been very helpful since Mr. Pepper and the others moved into the Crystal house (only I guess I should start calling it the Pepper house!), calling up to say they're going to the market and can they pick up anything at the store. Or dropping in with some homemade preserves, or cookies, or just to visit. That kind of thing.

I've got a heavier schedule this year than last, but I work a couple of hours every Saturday morning anyway over at Maple Ridge. Just because Mrs. Sherman and the others aren't there anymore doesn't mean the ones who are left don't need young people around.

My going there on Saturday mornings still upsets my Mom. She said, "Opie, I thought you had gotten this Maple Ridge business out of your system."

"You make it sound like I'm just getting over the measles or something."

"I want to remind you, Opie, that now you'll have

to study harder than ever if you plan to go to college. Grades really count now."

"I know that, Mom," I replied. I do know it. It's when you're in high school that it suddenly hits you how important your grades are. And before you know it, you've got to start thinking seriously about what you want to be later on in life.

"You should concentrate on some extra courses in English," she went on, "if you're going to be an English teacher." Notice how subtle my Mom is, the way she sneaked that in?

"No, Mom." For a minute I startled myself, I sounded so like my Dad when he's handed down a firm and final decision. "I don't want to be an English teacher. I don't want to be any kind of teacher."

She bit her lip and stared down at her plate. I knew she was very disappointed, but I couldn't help that. "And I'm not planning on becoming a social worker, either." She looked up again, feeling a little more hopeful, I guess.

"Opie," my Dad said, putting his fork down and pushing his dinner plate aside, "I'd appreciate it if you would stop telling us what you don't want to be and tell us what you do want to be."

"I want to be a lawyer. Like you."

His face flushed with pleasure. But when he spoke, his voice sounded calm and detached.

"I'm flattered, Opie. But becoming a lawyer is a long haul."

"It will take *years*," Mom interrupted. She sounded stunned.

I leaned toward my Dad, not trying to exclude my Mom or anything like that, but I knew my Dad would understand this better just now than my Mom would. "I never really thought about what you do before. Then I saw how you were able to help Mrs. Longwood. And then the others. Old people are so . . . so . . ."

"Defenseless?" my Dad suggested.

"Yes. Defenseless. They need someone who cares about them. Really cares. I've thought about it a lot lately. And that's what I want to do. Be a lawyer and specialize in helping old people get their rights."

"Years," my Mom repeated, her eyes glazing over.

My Dad reached over and patted her hand. "That's all right, Elizabeth," he comforted her. "We'll just take them one at a time. Won't we, Opie?"

It was after this conversation that my Dad told me how I'd matured this summer and I went and looked in the mirror to see if it showed in my face.

I guess there's nothing more to say, except that

I ran into Mrs. Humphreys the other day on the street. She was walking like one of her own red-ink letters, straight and tall, with her back starched. She stopped when she saw me.

"I will miss not having you in my class this year, Opie," she said. "What have you been up to this past summer?"

I laughed. "To tell you that, Mrs. Humphreys, I'd have to write a book."

"Why don't you?" she asked.

"Maybe I will," I called after her as she walked away.

Now that I think of it, maybe that's just exactly what I've done. Written a book on how I spent my summer vacation!